"**That shouldn't have happened,**" she said, her voice not much louder than a whisper.

"No. It shouldn't have." He didn't try to kiss her again.

She leaned her head against his chest. "It won't happen again."

"Count on it." He held her into the night as she fell into a troubled sleep. She clung to him, her body shaking, her head twisting back and forth as nightmares disturbed her slumber.

In the small hours of the morning, Pierce spooned her body against his, his gaze on the dying embers of the fire, his thoughts swirling around the shooting, the dirt bike, Roxanne and the bullet and wrapper they'd found in the cave.

Sleep escaped him with her body close to his and the wad of evidence in his pocket. The more he mulled over everything, the more dread filled his chest, crushing him with worry.

ELLE JAMES

THUNDER HORSE REDEMPTION

HARLEQUIN®

entertain, enrich, inspire™

This book is dedicated to the brave men and women who serve our country in the military, in law enforcement and as first responders. Their dedication to making our country and world a better place is selfless and commendable. Thank you.

Recycling programs
for this product may
not exist in your area.

ISBN-13: 978-0-373-74703-0

THUNDER HORSE REDEMPTION

ABOUT THE AUTHOR

A Golden Heart Award winner for Best Paranormal Romance in 2004, Elle James started writing when her sister issued a Y2K challenge to write a romance novel. She has managed a full-time job and raised three wonderful children, and she and her husband even tried their hands at ranching exotic birds (ostriches, emus and rheas) in the Texas Hill Country. Ask her, and she'll tell you what it's like to go toe-to-toe with an angry 350-pound bird! After leaving her successful career in information technology management, Elle is now pursuing her writing full-time. She loves building exciting stories about heroes, heroines, romance and passion. Elle loves to hear from fans. You can contact her at ellejames@earthlink.net or visit her website at www.ellejames.com.

Books by Elle James

CAST OF CHARACTERS

Pierce Thunder Horse—Lakota Indian, North Dakota rancher and FBI special agent assigned close to home at the Bismarck, North Dakota, branch office. In charge of the joint FBI and ATF investigation of a radical militia that ended in a deadly explosion.

Roxanne Carmichael—Last of the Carmichaels, independent and determined to keep her ranch afloat despite the bill collectors and attempts on her life. Blames her ex-fiancé, Pierce, for her brother's death in the explosion.

Deputy Shorty Duncan—County deputy in charge of the investigation of attempts on Roxanne Carmichael's life.

Jim Rausch—Roxanne's foreman, who has been with the Carmichael Ranch as long as Roxanne can remember.

Tuck Thunder Horse—Pierce's younger brother and an FBI special agent, back at the ranch in preparation for his wedding.

Dante Thunder Horse—Tuck's brother and a helicopter pilot for the North Dakota branch of U.S. Customs and Border Protection.

Maddox Thunder Horse—Rancher and oldest of the Thunder Horse brothers.

Ethan Mitchell—Roxanne's ranch hand with a sullen attitude and a murky past.

Toby Gentry—Young ranch hand new to the Carmichael Ranch.

Chapter One

His tailbone bruised, his thighs protesting the prolonged position, Pierce Thunder Horse shifted in the saddle. He hadn't been on a horse in over two months. There wasn't much call for FBI special agents to saddle up.

His typical visits to the family ranch were short. He loved his mother and brothers and would do anything for them, but the ranch held too many memories. Pierce didn't come home often—it hurt too much.

With Tuck's upcoming wedding, he couldn't avoid returning. The frenetic wedding planning served as a stark reminder of Pierce's own wedding that wasn't. When his mother had mentioned that someone should really check on the local herd of wild horses, Pierce had jumped at the chance to get away from the hubbub. But he'd ridden half of the day and had yet to find the herd. Soon he'd run out of Thunder Horse Ranch property and cross over onto the Carmichael Ranch.

Roxanne Carmichael.

The redheaded hellion, his former fiancée, had been the love of his life. She was also the one who'd called off their wedding when her brother Mason had died on the job, thanks to Pierce's mistake.

His chest tightened, his hands gripping the reins so tightly his knuckles whitened. Why couldn't he locate the blasted herd? He was out here to find the horses, not mull over what had happened.

Every member of the Thunder Horse family had a deep connection to the wild horses of the badlands. They always felt they needed to make sure the herd was healthy and thriving, even though official responsibility for the area's wild horses rested with the representative of the Bureau of Land Management—Roxanne. Damn! Had he really thought riding out to check on the herd would *stop* him from thinking about her? If so, he was a fool. Their love of the wild horses had brought them together.

Pierce remembered as if it had been yesterday the night he and Roxanne had saved a lost horse from a snowstorm. Roxanne had asked Pierce to help her bring the filly to her barn, where they'd nursed her to health and kept her warm and fed until the mare could be located and the two reunited. He'd known Roxanne for years, but that was the first time he'd realized what an amazing woman she'd become. It had been the beginning of their courtship. Eight months later, he'd asked her to marry him. And two months ago, she'd ended it.

Since then, he'd buried himself in his work to avoid the pain, the blame and the loss. He'd made it his objective to dodge memories and force to the back of his mind the date of his own wedding that hadn't happened and never would. But now that he was back at the Thunder Horse Ranch, Pierce had way too much time on his hands. Plus, the ranch carried too many memories—not just of Roxanne, but of Mason, who had been Pierce's friend since they were kids. The familiar settings only managed to dredge the painful memories back to the surface, a constant reminder of his failure professionally and personally.

A cold chill slithered down Pierce's back, chasing away the warmth of an early summer day in the North Dakota badlands.

He glanced up at the position of the sun as it dropped toward the horizon, his gaze lowering to the landscape. Nothing moved and only the sound of his horse's hooves clomping against the ground and the creak of leather interrupted his tumultuous thoughts.

With the sun so close to setting, Pierce wasn't going to find the herd and still have time to return to the ranch house before dark. Pierce had tugged his reins to the left, aiming the horse toward the barn, when a loud bang ripped through the silence.

Was that gunfire?

Bear, his stallion, danced beneath him, whinnying his fright.

Pierce spun back around and squinted against the setting sun, his gaze panning the prairie. Firing a weapon on the plains was rare but not unheard of, although it wasn't hunting season. Should he check it out? The sound had come from somewhere on the Carmichael Ranch. He hesitated, not at all anxious to cross over onto Carmichael property. He couldn't see anything, but his gut told him someone could be in trouble.

Another shot rang out.

Pierce nudged his horse.

Already nervous, Bear leaped forward, his legs stretching into a gallop, eating up the distance on the sparsely vegetated ground between him and whoever was shooting.

A smudge rose above the landscape, capturing Pierce's attention. From this distance, he couldn't tell if it was smoke or dust.

If the cloud was smoke, it meant a wildfire on the prairie.

The puff grew as Pierce approached. In the middle of the cloud of dirt rising from the dry prairie grass, a horse and rider emerged, riding hell-for-leather.

The rider leaned far forward, almost one with the horse, urging it faster.

As they neared, Pierce made out a small vehicle in pursuit. A dirt bike, the man steering it bent low over the handlebar.

As the horse and rider approached, the cowboy's hat flew from her head and a mass of deep auburn hair spilled out, flowing behind her.

Pierce couldn't mistake that red hair. It had to be Roxanne Carmichael, riding like her life depended on it.

His heart thumped, pressing hard against his ribs, making it difficult for him to breathe. Every instinct to protect what had once been his reared up in Pierce's consciousness. He spurred his mount to move faster.

Before he could reach her, another shot rang out and nicked the hindquarters of Roxanne's mare.

Already in a state of agitation, the horse bucked, then reared so suddenly that Roxanne toppled from the saddle, landing hard, flat on her back.

The mare took off, racing away from the dirt bike, leaving Roxanne at the mercy of the shooter.

The dirt bike, which had stopped while the driver fired his gun, now roared toward her again, speed increasing instead of decreasing, aiming directly for the woman lying on the ground.

At the last moment Roxanne rolled to the side, avoiding being hit.

Still too far away to intervene, Pierce pulled his rifle from the scabbard on his saddle and fired a round into the air. At the same time he dug his heels into Bear's flanks, pushing him to close the distance.

The shooter slowed and spun the bike to face Pierce, his dark helmet hiding his face. He lifted his hand, pointing it toward Pierce.

Sun glinted off the metal of the pistol he carried.

Pierce yanked Bear's reins to the side, forcing the animal to zigzag toward his target.

Another shot rang out.

Pierce answered, firing his rifle, careful to aim high to avoid hitting Roxanne. With the horse's movements the shot could go just about anywhere. All he might hope for was to scare the bastard away.

When Pierce didn't back down, the man on the bike spun his vehicle, the rear tire skidding sideways, kicking up dust in a dense cloud. The rider sped off across the prairie in the opposite direction. Within seconds, he disappeared over a rise, leaving a faint haze of dust in his wake.

Pierce raced to where Roxanne lay on the

ground, ignoring the instinct pressing him to pursue the rider. His own need to find and capture the man who'd shot at Roxanne mattered far less than making sure Roxanne herself wasn't badly injured. He jerked back hard on the reins, forcing his horse to rear and spin all in one motion. As soon as Bear's hooves touched ground, Pierce flung himself out of the saddle and ran toward Roxanne.

She lay flat on her back, cursing beneath her breath.

Pierce let out the gulp of air he'd been holding and chuckled. She couldn't be hurt badly if she had the energy and wherewithal to form coherent curses.

Roxanne pressed her fingers to the bridge of her nose, her eyes squeezed shut. "Did you get the license plate of the truck that hit me?" she asked.

Dropping to his knees beside her, Pierce ran his hands over her arms and legs, searching for fractured bones.

"I'm pretty sure there's nothing broken," she said, pushing his hands away as her eyes fluttered open. "Hello, Pierce." Her wide blue gaze was cool and wary. It hit Pierce like a gut punch to see her look at him with none of the warmth or love he'd cherished. He reminded himself that he was lucky she was even talking to him. After what he'd done, he wouldn't blame her if she never spoke to him again.

His chest tightened as his fingers slid up her arms. "Hello, Roxy. Are you okay?" He touched her gently, his hands moving around to the backs of her shoulders to help her sit up.

She leaned away from his touch then swayed and would have fallen back if Pierce hadn't reached behind her and steadied her with his arm. "Just had the wind knocked out of me in that fall. I'll be all right," she replied.

He leaned her against his chest to keep her from toppling over and further injuring herself, his heart clenching at the familiar aroma of her hair—honeysuckle and hay and the incongruous scent of copper, indicating fresh blood. When his right hand pulled away from her shoulder, it was red with her blood. "You've been injured, and not from the fall. Care to tell me how?"

"What?" She stared at the blood on his hand. "I'm bleeding?"

"Yes." He ripped off his denim shirt and the clean white T-shirt beneath, tearing a piece from the hem. He folded the soft fabric into a tight square wad and pressed it to the wound on her left shoulder, frowning as he evaluated the injury. It appeared to be just a nick, but it could have been so much worse.

"The shoulder doesn't hurt as bad as the back

of my head." She pressed her fingers to the back of her skull.

Pierce brushed her hand aside and parted her hair, finding a soft knot. "More than likely, you'll live. The shot to your shoulder was just a flesh wound. Are you up-to-date on your tetanus shot?"

"Had one a couple weeks ago." She snorted. "Stepped on a nail."

Pierce shook his head. "Sounds like you. You seem to follow trouble."

Roxanne sighed. "Yeah, that's me."

"What just happened here? Why was that man shooting at you?"

She started to shake her head, until the movement made her wince and clutch at the back of her head. "Remember the filly we rescued from the snowstorm two years ago?"

Pierce swallowed hard on the lump clogging his throat, remembering the night he'd fallen in love with Roxanne. "Sweet Jessie?"

"Yeah, that one." Roxanne opened her eyes wide and blinked several times. "I was following Sweet Jessie toward the canyon, hoping she'd lead me to the herd of wild horses, when I heard a shot from behind. I felt a sting and when I turned around, that dirt bike was behind me. I took off, he followed after me... You know the rest."

"Do you have any idea who the biker was?"

Pierce hadn't been able to make an identification, but it had been years since he'd lived full-time on the ranch. Roxanne would be more familiar with the locals—and their bikes—than him.

"No." She pinched the bridge of her nose again. "It's a bit blurry. I must have hit the ground pretty hard, just now. I was good until then."

Pierce stared into her eyes. "You could have a concussion. Can you get up on your own?"

"Absolutely." She pushed away from him and staggered to her feet. Then she swayed and her knees buckled, tipping her over into Pierce.

Pierce straightened, then hooked his arm beneath her knees and scooped her up, settling her against his chest. He glanced around, searching for Bear. He gave a short, sharp whistle.

The stallion trotted toward him, snorting and tossing his mane, still hyped up from the mad dash to save Roxanne.

"Easy, *Mato Cikala*." Little Bear. Pierce spoke low and slow in his native Lakota language as he approached the spooked horse, maintaining eye contact with the animal the entire time.

Ultimately, the stallion calmed, his dancing hooves settling to a stop in the dry prairie grass.

Pierce lifted Roxanne up onto the saddle, seating her sideways. He placed her hands on the saddle horn and said, "Hold on."

Roxanne's lips tightened. "I know how to ride a horse."

"I know," he said, before he placed his boot in the stirrup and mounted behind her. Then he slid into the saddle, lifting her to sit across his lap.

"This is silly. I can handle a horse by myself."

"You may be fully capable, but I don't intend to walk all the way to the ranch."

"My mare—"

"Is halfway back to the barn by now." He bit hard on his tongue to keep from saying more. He knew she didn't want to be anywhere near him, so the least he could do was make the trip as unobtrusive as possible. Besides, when they weren't talking—arguing—he could almost pretend that things were the way they used to be. Pretend she didn't hate him...and that he didn't hate himself.

The stubborn look on her face didn't match the glazed look in her eyes and the way she swayed as she sat there alone.

His heart clinched. "Try not to argue, for once."

"I DON'T ARGUE," SHE muttered, her body naturally leaning against his, despite her better judgment.

With her brain somewhat fuzzy, she had to work to remind herself that Pierce Thunder Horse wasn't someone she could trust.

When she realized he was headed away from

her ranch, Roxanne frowned. "You're going the wrong way."

"I'm taking you home with me."

"I can't go home with you! Some maniac is out there on a dirt bike shooting up every rider he sees—I need to get home so I can call the sheriff and tell him what happened. Then I need to check on my horse and make sure she got back safe and isn't badly hurt. And when that's done, I'll need to saddle back up to go check on Sweet Jessie— I think the bullet that winged me might have hit her, too, but I didn't have a chance to check."

"You can call the sheriff from our house— for all the good that will do—and you can call your foreman to check on your horse. Jim knows your stables as well as you do, and he'll be able to take care of the mare if anything's wrong. As for Sweet Jessie, I'll send one of my brothers back to check on her. But right now, you've got a bullet hole in your shoulder, and every sign of a concussion. You need to go where people can take care of you."

"And you think *you* can take care of me?" As soon as the words came out, they both flinched. She knew it was a low blow to throw Mason in Pierce's face, even if he *had* fallen short on his promise to keep her brother safe. They both knew what Pierce had done—he'd never offered any excuses for what had happened to Mason, not even when she'd begged him to explain.

"It's my responsibility to personally verify the status of the wild horses," she said, choosing to change the subject. She glanced behind them as if she could see to where she'd left Sweet Jessie. "I can't just let someone else take care of it." *I've got responsibilities, too,* she wanted to say—but didn't.

"The sooner you stop arguing, the sooner you can get fixed up enough to leave. Until then, you're on *my* horse and we're going to *my* house."

She stared up into his face and recognized that Thunder Horse stubborn streak in the tightness of his jaw. He wasn't going to budge on the matter.

The ache in her head intensified and her shoulder burned where she'd been nicked. She willed herself to be stronger, squeezing closed her eyes as a wave of nausea washed over her. When she opened her eyes, her vision was no less blurry, maybe having something to do with the tears of frustration threatening to fall.

Dear God, she refused to cry in front of Pierce. She'd already spent the past two months crying when no one was looking.

With her horse gone, the shooter still at large and herself just about too tired and bruised to muster up the energy to do anything at all, she decided not to argue with the man. Instead, she clamped shut her lips and tried to keep as far away from Pierce as possible. A difficult task, considering she was sitting in his lap.

After a few minutes, the sway of the horse lulled her into a daze. Giving up the fight, she leaned into his body and stayed there the rest of the ride back to the Thunder Horse Ranch.

The scent of leather and denim and the familiar earthy, musky male aroma set her heart beating faster and heat radiating throughout her body, reminding her of better times and of all they'd lost.

If she hadn't called off the engagement then she and Pierce would have married by now. They might even have had a baby on the way. She'd loved Pierce so much, had been so sure that she'd finally found someone she could count on, someone who could be a real partner in her life as well as a lover. Losing that hope had hurt. It *still* hurt.

A sob rose in her throat, choking off the air to her lungs. Her head aching with each passing mile, Roxanne stiffened and tried to move away from Pierce.

The arm around her tightened, pinning her. Short of making a big fuss and possibly falling off the horse, Roxanne had no choice but to stay put.

Rather than relive their final days as an engaged couple, Roxanne forced herself to think through what had just happened. "What do you think that man was after?" she wondered out loud.

"I don't know, but he seemed pretty determined to shoot you." Pierce's grip tightened on the reins.

The stallion danced sideways, seemingly confused by his rider's instruction to slow.

A slight movement of Pierce's legs, and loosening the reins, set the horse in a forward motion again.

"If someone wanted to shoot me, why would he wait until I was out in the canyon? There are easier ways to find me, in places where he could have gotten close enough to get a much better shot."

Pierce liked that thought even less if the way he tensed was any indication, but before he could reply, the stallion beneath them stumbled, jolting Roxanne. She winced, pressing a hand to the back of her skull. "Ouch. Must have hit my head harder than I thought."

"I'll get the doctor to come out as soon as I've got you settled."

"I'm fine. Just a flesh wound and a bump on the noggin. I'll be back in the saddle by morning."

"Not if you have a concussion." His voice was firm, unyielding. "The doctor will have to clear you to my satisfaction before I let you leave the ranch."

"Hey, get this straight, mister." She poked him in the chest. "The decisions about what I can and cannot do are between me and the doctor. You've got no part in them, or in anything else that has to do with me."

She recognized the mulish expression on his face and knew what he'd say before he even opened his mouth. "When you don't know what's good for you then somebody has to step in."

"*You're* not good for me—we're not good for each other. We can't even ride a couple of miles of trail together without fighting." She took a deep breath, forcing her voice to sound calm, collected. "Just let me go home, Pierce. I'm not your problem anymore, and I can take care of myself. I've been running a ranch by myself for years. I think I can make my own decisions."

Another jolt and the pain reverberating around the inside of her skull made her cringe. Well, darn it all. Why did she have to be so weak in front of the one man she'd sworn to never show an ounce of vulnerability again?

"Look," Pierce said. "I don't want you at the ranch any more than you want to be there. But I won't let you go home until the doc says you can."

Her chest tightened at his harsh words. Once they could barely stand to be apart. Now they could barely stand to be together. Too much had happened. Irreversible actions and words with permanent consequences. "Okay, I'll stay until the doctor can convince you that I'm all right. Which I am."

Roxanne didn't relish the idea of being at the Thunder Horse Ranch with Pierce there. She'd been over a couple times to meet Tuck's fiancée and get measured for her bridesmaid dress, but she'd left as soon as possible to avoid any chance of running into Pierce.

Why did he have to be the one to find her out in the canyon? Why couldn't it have been Tuck, or one of Pierce's other brothers? Why did her already horrible day have to sink to the new low of having to depend on the man who'd encouraged her brother to join the FBI and then let him die in that explosion?

What had happened had been inexcusable and irreversible. She knew that for sure. Not because of the FBI—the official word they had given her was that Mason's death had been ruled unavoidable.

No. Roxanne knew Pierce was responsible for her brother's death because that was what he had told her himself.

Chapter Two

Pierce insisted on carrying Roxanne into the cavernous great room of the Thunder Horse Ranch house, despite her objections. The feel of her body against his brought back so many memories he could barely breathe.

"I can walk, really." She kicked her legs and pushed against his chest. "Let me down." Twin flags of color rose in her cheeks as he entered the room where two of his brothers and his mother stood gaping at them.

Stopping just inside the entry, Pierce braced himself for the onslaught of questions his family was sure to ask.

His mother was the first to remember her manners. "Roxy, good to see you, sweetie," she said as though it was an everyday occurrence for her son to stroll in carrying his ex-fiancée. "Oh, dear, is that blood?" She lifted a hand to her own cheek, her eyes widening. "For goodness' sake, Pierce, let her have the lounge chair," she commanded.

"I'll get some coffee. Maddox, you call Doc Taylor. Pierce, give Dante the details of what happened in case you need his help with anything else."

Pierce smiled despite the gravity of the situation. Though thin and petite, his mother had a will of iron, with a bossy streak to match. She didn't hesitate to tell her boys what to do, no matter that they were all grown men who now towered over her small frame.

"Yeah, what happened?" Dante planted himself in front of Pierce, his gaze taking in the torn shirt and bloodstains. "Are you hurt, too?" His arms crossed over his chest, his eyebrows knitting in a fierce frown, clearly ready to take on anyone who might be a danger to their family.

"I'm fine, Roxanne's the only one hurt," Pierce said. "Found her out on the northernmost corner of the ranch." Pierce's jaw tightened. "Someone was using her for target practice."

"The chair?" Roxanne tipped her head toward the chair Pierce's mother had indicated. "At least put me down. It's not like I can't walk."

"Yeah, why are you carrying her?" Dante asked. "Are her legs injured, too?"

"She's not all that steady on her feet. Her horse threw her and she hit her head. I think she might have a concussion." Pierce relented and eased Roxanne into the chair.

"What were you doing out by the canyons?" Dante asked, turning his focus to Roxanne.

"I was checking on the wild horses." Roxanne sat in the chair, her chin tipped upward, one hand feeling the back of her head. She winced. "I was following Sweet Jessie. I found her by the watering hole near North Canyon. When I went down to check on her, I heard a loud bang. Something stung my arm and almost knocked me out of the saddle. Whatever nicked me, hit Jessie—most likely in the shoulder, but I couldn't say for sure. She might have tripped or been hit because I think I saw her drop to the ground before my mount took off. The shooter came after me. That's when Pierce found us."

Dante swore. "Did you see who it was?"

Roxanne sighed. "No. I didn't. He was on a dirt bike in full-coverage gear, including a helmet."

Tuck entered the room, carrying his baby girl, Lily. "What's going on?"

His beautiful blonde fiancée, Julia Anderson, followed him. When she noticed Roxanne on the chair, she hurried around to stand in front of her. "Good Lord, Roxanne, are you all right?"

Pierce frowned. Apparently the two women had already met while Pierce had been wrapping up his previous assignment in Bismarck. What else had he missed?

Roxanne smiled. "Don't worry, Julia, I'll be

fine for the wedding." She pushed against the seat cushions, preparing to stand.

Julia laid a hand on her uninjured shoulder. "I'm not worried about the wedding. I want to know what happened to you. Holy smokes, you're bleeding." Julia reached out to touch Roxanne's other arm where Pierce had wrapped his shirt around her injury.

"It's nothing. Just a flesh wound." Roxanne shot a glance toward Pierce. "Pierce patched me up and it's not bleeding so badly anymore."

The baby, clearly picking up on the distress in Julia's voice, leaned away from Tuck, reaching for her mother.

Julia turned automatically to play with Lily's hands, rather than take the baby, keeping most of her attention on Roxanne. The baby giggled and buried her face in Tuck's shirt.

A sharp pang tugged at Roxanne's gut. She knew things hadn't been easy for Tuck and Julia. A quickie Vegas-style marriage—followed by an even quicker divorce—had separated the couple only hours after they'd met. Tuck hadn't even known their brief union had resulted in a daughter until a few weeks earlier. But now that their differences had been worked out, the little family looked so natural and beautiful together, full of so much love and happiness.

"It doesn't make any sense," Pierce's oldest

brother, Maddox, said as he paced the floor. "Who would want to shoot at you?"

"It doesn't make sense to *you?*" Roxanne snorted softly. "I was the one being shot at and it makes no more sense to me. Maybe he wasn't shooting at me at all. He could have been aiming for the horse for a little target practice." Her lips tightened. "There are idiots out there that get a kick out of killing defenseless animals."

Pierce's jaw clenched. "They're idiots, all right, but they're not stupid enough to shoot at the horses in front of a potentially hostile witness. And it's not like he didn't realize you were there. If you were in between the shooter and Sweet Jessie, he had to be shooting at you."

Maddox inhaled and let his breath out slowly. "I'm glad it was only a flesh wound." His shoulders pushed back and he looked around the room at his younger brothers. "We'd better get out there and see if we can find out who did this." He turned to Dante and Tuck. "You two take the truck. I'll take the four-wheeler."

"I'm going by horse." Pierce straightened, anger building with each breath he took. Someone had shot at Roxanne, tried to run over her and almost killed her. The bastard needed to be found. If he'd been faster, smarter…maybe he could have taken the guy into custody back in the canyon. It was his fault Roxanne was still in danger. Pierce should have gone after him while he'd had the chance.

Dante grabbed his cowboy hat from the coat tree in the hallway. "We have to find whoever did this. The prairie and canyons are dangerous enough without people shooting at one of us."

"Who would want to hurt Roxanne?" Tuck handed the baby to Julia, who nestled Lily into the crook of her arm, a frown marring her brow.

"I don't know, but we sure as hell are going to find out." Pierce clamped his hat on his head, grabbed a box of bullets from the gun cabinet and headed for his father's office. For what it was worth, he placed a call to the sheriff's department. When the dispatcher came on, Pierce explained the situation and the approximate location.

The dispatcher promised the sheriff's department would be out to investigate as soon as they had a deputy available. Pierce hung up, shrugging. He'd done the right thing by reporting the incident, but he didn't have a whole lot of faith or respect for the local sheriff. The man still stood by the theory that Pierce's father had fallen from his horse and died of head injuries. Pierce and his brothers disagreed. No way their father had fallen from his horse. The man could ride before he learned to walk. But the sheriff refused to put in the effort to find the truth. And Pierce refused to let Roxanne's safety depend on that kind of man. Whether she liked it or not, he still considered her *his* responsibility. He wouldn't let her down, not this time. Not again.

Pierce grabbed a couple of walkie-talkies from a shelf and emerged from his father's office.

At the same time Amelia Thunder Horse re-entered the living room, carrying a large tray filled with thermoses of coffee, and plastic bags filled with sandwiches and trail mix. She eyed the box of bullets but didn't say anything about them. "No one's leaving without food. You never know what's going to happen out there on the plains or in the canyons. They didn't name it the badlands for nothing."

Pierce tossed a walkie-talkie to Maddox, grabbed a plastic bag of trail mix and one with a sandwich from the tray, snagged a thermos, kissed his mother's cheek and headed for the door. "Thanks, Mother."

She called out after him, *"Wakan Tanka kici un."* May the Great Spirit bless you.

He smiled, a tug of nostalgia tightening his chest. His mother didn't often use the Lakota language his father had taught her and all of his sons. Only when a greater need arose.

In the barn, Pierce removed the saddle from Bear, rubbed him down and settled him in a stall with feed. He led his own stallion, Cetan, out of his stall, threw a saddle over his back and cinched it. Pierce was guiding the horse out into the barnyard when a voice called out.

"I'm going with you."

Pierce turned toward the sound, his pulse quickening, his jaw growing rigid.

Roxanne stood with her feet planted wide, hands fisted on her jean-clad hips—more beautiful than he remembered and just as stubbornly determined.

"We don't need your help." Pierce turned his back on the woman and led the horse away from the barn door. "Besides, isn't the doctor on his way to check out your noggin?"

Roxanne strode for the barn. "I've been falling off horses since I was five years old—Doc's not going to tell me anything about concussions that I don't already know. But don't forget, I wasn't the only one injured. While you boys play detective, someone needs to check on Sweet Jessie, and her foal. I'm the local contact for the Bureau of Land Management when it comes to those horses. It's my—"

"Responsibility." Pierce turned back. "And it's *my* responsibility to catch that madman with a gun before he gets a chance to come after you again. You're staying."

"I'm *not* your responsibility, and you don't get to decide where I go. Maddox said I could ride

Sassy." She marched into the barn and grabbed a bridle from a nail on the wall.

"Did the fact escape you that you were the target of a shooter?"

"No, it did not." She squared her shoulders, standing taller. "I wasn't prepared before. I'm aware now and will take precautions."

"And how will you do that?" His gaze panned her lithe form. "You aren't carrying any kind of protection, are you? Where's your rifle?"

"I don't carry one. Besides, you have one." She frowned. "Look, Pierce, I'm being sensible. I could have snuck off on my own once you were gone, but instead I'm going with you. I'm willing to be careful, I'm willing to take precautions, but I'm *not* willing to sit around and do nothing when there's so much that needs to be done. Accept that I'm going and stop wasting precious time by arguing. It'll be dark soon."

She held his gaze a moment longer, then disappeared into a stall and emerged leading Sassy, the sorrel mare.

Pierce didn't wait around to bicker with the confounded woman. He didn't want to see Roxanne; he wanted the hell away from her, especially when fire blazed in her beautiful eyes and she stood so defiantly.

Planting his foot in the stirrup, he swung up into his saddle and yanked the stallion around to the north. Named after the Lakota word for hawk, Cetan could outrun even the swiftest of the wild horses in the canyon. He could easily outdistance any of the other horses in the barn, if Pierce chose to let him have his head.

But it would be foolish to expend the horse's energy when they had a long ride ahead of them. Instead of galloping off into the distance, Pierce nudged the stallion into a canter. That way, Roxanne wouldn't have any trouble catching up with him. He still didn't like the idea of her riding out while the gunman was still at large, but the idea of her sticking close and letting him protect her was a hell of a lot better than having her ride out alone.

In the short time they'd been in the ranch house, dark clouds had rolled in. The weather in North Dakota could change at the drop of a hat. Thunder rumbled long and low in the west. *Wakan Tanka* grew angry. Perhaps the Great Spirit reached out to punish those who brought violence to the people and the creatures of the plains.

The approaching storm reflected Pierce's mood. He growled under his breath. Sure, he'd expected to see Roxanne as part of the wedding party. She and Tuck were the same age and had been friends throughout high school. They had been like brother and sister.

Despite the differences between Pierce and Roxanne, Pierce couldn't deny Tuck's request to have Roxanne as one of Julia's bridesmaids.

He'd told himself that he'd be fine seeing her again, but he'd been wrong. Time hadn't healed old wounds, as his mother always liked to say. Nothing could cure death. Roxanne had made it clear that when her brother had died, she wanted nothing more to do with Pierce. No wedding, no future…nothing. Even though he knew it was no more than he deserved, it still made his gut twist just to think about it.

All the old feelings he'd had for her hadn't waned one bit. No amount of dating or bedding other women would wipe Roxanne from his mind. He'd barely even tried, the wounds to his heart still too fresh. He told himself he preferred to be alone. No, he *deserved* to be alone.

Truth was, no woman measured up to Roxanne and he'd failed her so completely, the damage could never be healed.

At the approaching thunder of hooves, Cetan pranced to the side.

Pierce pulled back on the reins, but the stallion would have none of it. His competitive spirit wouldn't let another horse catch up or move ahead of him. He arched his back, kicked his hind legs into the air and would have thrown a less experienced rider.

Accustomed to surprising mood swings in the horses he'd tamed from the wild herds of the canyons, Pierce rode out the rough bucking and brought Cetan to a halt.

Roxanne approached with a hint of a smirk curling the corners of her lips.

Pierce's back teeth ground together. When she pulled in beside him, he eased control on Cetan's reins and let the stallion take the lead in a steady trot. Pierce didn't speak or acknowledge her presence. He was afraid of what he might say. Yet, he kept an eye on Roxanne, just in case. She was hurt, and she was in danger. Even though she hated him, he knew he couldn't live with himself unless he kept her safe.

ROXANNE'S GAZE BORED into Pierce's back. She should have ridden with Dante and Tuck in the truck. But she knew where she was most comfortable. When trouble struck the badlands of North Dakota, Roxanne preferred to be in the saddle. Besides, she was more likely to find Sweet Jessie and her foal off the beaten path, and they were her priority right now.

The fact that *she* had been injured, along with Sweet Jessie, wasn't something Roxanne let herself think about. She didn't know why anyone would choose to target her—or if he would try to attack her again—but sitting around and thinking about it would drive her crazy. With all the problems she'd been having with the ranch and her finances, the thought of another disaster in her life threatened to crack her self-control. The only way she knew to deal with the strain was to focus on something else—a problem she could fix.

Checking on the horses fit the bill, even if it meant riding with her ex-fiancé.

She'd avoided Pierce since her brother's death. The only time she saw him was from a distance when they happened to be in Medora, the small town where she purchased supplies. She had noticed that Pierce hadn't been home much since the explosion, and why should he? His work with the FBI kept him busy. Just like it had kept Mason busy when Pierce had lured him into that danger-filled world.

A booming clap of thunder shook the earth and air around her. The mare beneath her skittered sideways, tossing her head in the air with a frightened whinny.

Roxanne glanced at the incoming storm, doubt tugging at her gut. Maybe they should have waited until the following day to be out on the prairie. With no trees within sight, that left the two horses and riders as the tallest spires within miles—lightning rods for what looked like a nasty storm about to break over the landscape. Easy targets for a determined shooter, should he choose to return. But no, she wasn't letting herself think about that now. She'd set a mission for herself, and she wasn't going home until it was completed.

A flash of lightning snaked across the sky, followed closely by an answering rumble. Sassy pulled against the reins and swung back toward the barn and shelter from the oncoming storm.

Roxanne struggled to turn the horse in the direction Pierce and his stallion rode. They had to get to the watering hole and find Sweet Jessie and her foal before wolves or two-legged snakes claimed their lives. The rain would wash away the horse tracks...and the tracks of the dirt bike the Thunder Horse brothers would use to try to track down her shooter.

Ahead, Pierce sat tall in the saddle, his shoulders broad, his dark Lakota hair hanging down just below his collar, straight, thick and jet-black. The cowboy hat on his head shielded his eyes from what little light shone around the approaching cloud bank. Every time Pierce glanced behind him, Roxanne's heart flipped, stuttered and burst into a frantic pattering.

Damn the man. He'd always had that effect on her. When would she ever get over him? No man had ever captured her heart or imagination like Pierce Thunder Horse.

The truck with two of the other Thunder Horse

brothers passed them, followed soon by the four-wheeler. They honked and swung wide of Pierce and Roxanne, kicking up a cloud of dust from the dry prairie floor.

Roxanne settled into a bone-jarring canter, slow enough to conserve the horse's energy. If they had to go down into the canyon to find Sweet Jessie and her foal, the rain would make the trail even more dangerous than it already was.

Sassy would need all her strength for a coordinated and sure-footed descent.

As they neared the watering hole, Roxanne let out a sigh, half-relieved when she didn't find the wild mare's body in the dirt. The wound mustn't have been too bad, if she was able to get up and leave the area. Still, Roxanne wanted to gauge for herself.

Pierce paused briefly at the watering hole to check for hoofprints and tire tracks, and to compare notes with his brothers.

Roxanne urged her mare slowly toward the canyon's rim, her gaze darting right and left as well as scanning the ground. Having been shot at once made her paranoid. Every noise caused her to jump. She tried to force herself to focus. The brothers were taking care of the shooter—Roxanne's job was to take care of the wild horses. She couldn't let herself get distracted from that. If she did, she'd be reminded how vulnerable and frightened she felt at the thought of a gunman on her trail.

Sweet Jessie had been shot by the pond. The herd had to have been close by at the time of the shooting. Noise from the gunshot would have sent them into the canyon to hide.

In the dirt leading away from the watering hole, Roxanne discovered a trail of dark brown dots. Dried blood and hoofprints. At first they headed for the canyon, but the prints veered south before reaching the canyon's edge. Unfortunately, where Sweet Jessie's prints headed south, another, smaller set of hoofprints led directly to the canyon.

"The foal and mare are separated." Roxanne glanced across at Pierce as he came abreast. "The little one won't stand a chance if she doesn't find her mother soon."

At the edge of the gorge, Roxanne paused, searching for the trailhead where the horses would have dropped down into the canyon below.

"Are you trying to get shot again?" Pierce angled his horse in front of hers. "You're exposed here on the edge of the canyon. If someone wanted to shoot you once, wouldn't you think they might be interested in shooting at you again?"

"And like I said to you before, if someone wanted to shoot me, there are better places for them to try than here where there's next to no cover to get a good position—especially now that I'm surrounded by angry-looking men with guns." She straightened her shoulders, her gaze darting toward the canyon below. "I refuse to run scared. There's a foal down there who will die without her mother. Lead, follow or get out of my way."

Pierce's brows dipped. "You're a stubborn woman. Anywhere along the trail is easy pickings if someone is down there in the canyon aiming up."

"Do you see any tire tracks leading down into the canyon?"

Pierce leaned over in the saddle, scanning the trailhead. "No. But this might not be the trail he used to get down there."

"You do see horse tracks, don't you?"

"Yes."

Roxanne raised her gaze to the sky again. "If we don't hurry, it won't matter. The rain will keep us from finding the foal. She could die and no one will care but me."

He shifted in his saddle, glancing out across the gorge, squinting. Finally he faced her. "Damn it, Roxanne, I care."

She waved her hand toward the trail, choosing to ignore his statement. "Then let's go."

"Wait here." Pierce took off at a trot toward his

brothers. Over his shoulder he called out. "And I mean wait."

Roxanne's gaze followed him.

Pierce conferred with his brothers and returned, reining in beside her and her mare. "They want to stay up top and continue searching for clues as to who the shooter might be before the rain washes away any evidence, but Maddox will cover us while we go down."

"Good." She didn't wait for him. Pressing her heels into Sassy's flanks, she clucked her tongue and spoke softly to the horse as she picked her way down the steep and narrow trail.

Roxanne focused on the path ahead, refusing to look to her side where the ground dropped away in a slope too steep for man or beast. If a shooter popped off a round, he wouldn't even have to hit her. The noise alone could cause her horse to spook and toss her or, worse, tumble down the steep slope with her. And even without the shooter, if her mount took one faulty step, both horse and rider would plummet to the bottom of the canyon with nothing to slow their fall.

Her breath wedging in her throat, Roxanne clung to the saddle horn, her fingers light on the reins, giving the horse her head. Roxanne's feet dug into the stirrups as she leaned back in the saddle to keep from pitching forward. Sassy picked her way to the bottom at her own pace.

About halfway down, the sky opened, rain gushing from it like a fire hose spraying down full blast.

Blinded by the torrent, Roxanne could do nothing but hold on and pray Sassy remained sure-footed as the trail turned slippery and more treacherous by the minute.

Not until the path leveled out and the canyon floor rose up to meet them did Roxanne release the breath she'd been holding and push the hair out of her face to glance behind her.

Cetan descended, easing his way down the last few feet of the narrow trail. Rain dripped from the edges of Pierce's cowboy hat, his face set in stone beneath the brim.

"We'll be lucky to find the foal in this," Roxanne called out as Pierce reined in beside her.

"We're here, we might as well try." His heels pressed into his horse's sides and he headed north along the base of the cliffs rising up beside him.

Her head down, Roxanne wished she'd taken time to grab a cowboy hat at the Thunder Horse Ranch. Hers had been lost earlier in her wild ride to get away from the shooter. She could barely see through the rain running down her face. Sassy fell in step behind Cetan, seemingly content to let the larger horse lead as they pushed forward.

Roxanne followed the man she'd sworn to hate for the rest of her life. Weak and tired from the long ride and the injuries she'd sustained from being shot and thrown, she did something she swore she'd never do again. She let the tears she'd been holding back for two months, mingle with the rain coursing down her cheeks.

If Pierce looked behind him, all he'd see was a pathetically wet woman with water streaming down her face on the back of a bedraggled horse. He would never know she cried.

After riding in the torrential downpour for several hundred yards, Pierce's horse tossed his head into the air and took off.

Startled by the sudden movement, Sassy danced sideways.

Blinded by the rain in her eyes, Roxanne scrubbed a hand across her face and peered ahead.

Several yards in front of Pierce a blurry shadow darted toward the shallow river cutting through the center of the narrow canyon. The foal? She could only hope so. Because if it was the shooter, she didn't know what she could do to protect herself.

Roxanne dug her heels into Sassy's flanks. The horse leaped forward as the sequence of events unfolded before her.

With one hand, Peirce held the reins, while his other hand reached for the rope hanging from the side of his saddle. His arm rose high above his head, the rope swinging in a wide loop. When Pierce launched the lasso, the ring dropped over the head of the small horse that appeared too young to be weaned.

Pierce's horse dug his hooves into the slippery soil, sliding forward with the force of the foal's tug on the rope.

As soon as the two beasts came to an unsteady halt, Pierce dropped from his saddle and raced toward the filly.

Roxanne reached them at the same time, slipping from her horse's back to the ground. She stumbled, regained her footing and ran forward, flinging her arms around the filly's neck to add her weight to Pierce's hold until the frightened animal calmed.

Pierce spoke to her in a deep, monotone voice, whispering the words of his forefathers, the Lakota language rolling smoothly off his tongue.

Not only did it soothe the frightened animal, it helped steady Roxanne's racing heart.

The foal finally settled, eyes still wide, nostrils flaring, body quivering, her ribs expanding with each frantic breath she took. At least she didn't try to break free of Pierce and Roxanne. A fierce surge of triumph filled Roxanne. Despite everything that was wrong—and increasingly dangerous—in her life, at least they'd managed to do this. They'd found and caught the foal, which felt like the first thing that had gone right in her life in way too long.

With the lighting flashing above the canyons and the thunder booming against the rocky cliffs, Roxanne stared across the filly's neck at the man she'd once loved. Their gazes met and held.

Sometime during the struggle with the young horse, Pierce had lost his cowboy hat. Black hair lay plastered to his head, his high cheekbones standing out, glistening in the rain. His eyes glowed so darkly Roxanne couldn't fathom what thoughts hid behind their inky depths.

All she knew was that her traitorous heart was not her own and hadn't been since the day she'd fallen in love with Pierce Thunder Horse.

Chapter Three

Pierce's heartbeat thundered along with the storm-ravaged sky as he gazed into Roxanne's eyes. It took all his willpower and a little help from *Wakan Tanka,* the Great Spirit, to break eye contact and focus on the task ahead. "We need to get the filly back to the ranch."

Roxanne glanced back in the direction from which they'd come. "The trail will be too slippery to get out of the canyon."

Pierce knew that, but he couldn't bring himself to stay with Roxanne any longer than necessary. "We have to try."

She shook her head. "No. We can't risk it. Not when the filly is so scared to begin with. At least not until the rain stops. It wouldn't be safe for us or our horses, either."

He knew she was right. "Get the halter hanging on the side of my saddle."

"Are you sure you have her?"

The filly bucked beneath his hold. Pierce refused to let go, his hands clamped around her neck. "Yes," he said between gritted teeth. "Get it."

Roxanne raced for the saddle, snatched the halter and a lead rope and returned at a slower, more steady pace so as to not spook the foal. She slipped the straps over the pony's nose and buckled the clasp behind her ear. Once she had the lead snapped onto the ring at the side, she nodded. "I've got her."

Slowly, Pierce let go of his hold around the filly's neck.

Immediately, the young horse reared.

Roxanne dug her heels into the ground, but the little horse dragged her through the mud anyway.

Pierce grabbed Roxanne around the middle and held on. With his other hand he reached for the lead rope.

Together, they wrestled the filly to a standstill, Pierce's hand closing around Roxanne's on the rope.

Not until he had the foal under control did Pierce note how close he was to Roxanne. Her drenched body pressed against his, the cold rain doing nothing to cool the heat pooling in his loins.

His hand curled around her hip, dragging her closer. He sucked in a deep breath, inhaling the scent of honeysuckle, the knot in his gut tightening. "Why did you have to come back into my life?"

Her body stiffened, the hand beneath his convulsing around the rope. "Trust me, I had no intention of crossing paths with you." Despite her harsh words, her voice shook.

"Then get away, and stay away from me." He pushed her away from his body, both hands wrapping around the lead rope.

"I can't, until this storm clears." With her back to him, she walked several steps away, then swung around to face him. Hands perched on her hips, her blue eyes flashed through the rain running down her face. "Pending clear skies and dry trails, we're stuck with each other. Not my choice, but I'll deal with it. For now, we need to find shelter until this storm blows over."

"Got anything in mind?" The foal bucked and Pierce gritted his teeth, holding on.

"There are some caves somewhere around here. My brother…" Her voice caught and she looked away. "We used to camp close by when we fished in the river." She grabbed her horse's reins and Cetan's and left Pierce standing there holding on to the filly.

He could choose to follow or continue arguing with the rocks in the rain. For a moment he debated staying put, convinced the cold rain seemed a whole lot cozier than holing up in a cave with an angry ex-fiancée. One look at his charge and he knew the filly deserved better. Besides, until the shooter was caught, Pierce knew he wasn't going to be comfortable having his eyes off Roxanne for long, no matter how hard it was to look at her and know that she'd never be his again. Pierce fell in step behind Roxanne and the two horses, dragging the stubborn little beast with him.

Within fifteen minutes of trudging through rain and mud, Roxanne located the first of a series of caves she'd spent many summers camping in with her brother and father. The memories they evoked made a cold lump rise in her throat, reminding her why she could never forgive Pierce Thunder Horse.

A jagged crevice, wide enough for two horses to stand abreast, allowed them to enter without ducking, bending or otherwise forcing the animals through. The opening also allowed a moderate amount of light inside. The cave's interior, carved out of solid rock through years of erosion, was the size of a barn.

Getting the filly inside took a little more time and patience, but with Roxanne's help, Pierce maneuvered the frightened animal through the passageway, tying her to a boulder large enough to anchor her.

"I'll be right back. I need to radio my brothers and let them know we're okay and will stay here until the rain lets up." He went back through the crevice to stand at the opening of the cave, far enough away from the horses the static wouldn't bother them. The distance from Roxanne helped him to think as he made contact with his brothers. Too bad he couldn't come up with any solutions to keep Roxanne safe and also far, far away from him.

TIRED AND COLD TO THE bone, Roxanne dragged the saddle from Sassy and let it fall to the floor. What had happened to her strength? She felt as weak as a kitten. Determined to pull her own weight, she lugged the saddle up onto a large rock to dry. She used the saddle blanket to rub down the horse, then stretched the damp blanket over another rock.

Pierce reentered the cave.

"They didn't try to come down the trail after us, did they?" Roxanne asked.

"No. But they were about to when I called. They'd been searching the area and were fortunate enough to find some bullet casings before the rain hit. I told them where we were, and sent them back to the ranch. They're not going to find anything else out there in this weather. They'll contact the sheriff's department and let them know about the casings."

Once both horses were cared for, Roxanne

trudged her way through the darkness, searching for anything they could use for firewood. When she and her brother had last been inside the cave years ago, they'd left enough fuel to burn for the next visit, knowing firewood was scarce on the plains.

In the shadows farther away from the entrance, she located the ring of stones they'd arranged for the fire. That was expected. Less expected was what she found at the center of the circle—charred firewood, discarded cans and plastic wrappers that had definitely *not* come from her or Mason.

"Someone has used this cave. By the looks of this trash, fairly recently." Roxanne lifted a plastic wrapper and something shone brightly beneath, catching the little bit of light from the cave's access. "Interesting." She pushed the object out of the dirt. "It's a bullet." From the shooter? Well, who else could it be? This cave was on Carmichael property, and there certainly wasn't anyone who had permission to be using it.

Pierce caught her hand as she reached for the shiny metal. "Don't. We might be able to lift prints. And let me have that plastic wrapper." He tore the tail of his shirt off and picked up the unexploded round and the wrapper using the piece of fabric, tucking the wad into his jeans pocket.

Roxanne rearranged the ring of stones, searching for any other items of interest. "You think the man who camped here is the same man who shot at me?"

His lips thinned into a straight line. "We won't know until the state crime lab can perform the forensics on the casing and compare it to the ones my brothers found."

"Hopefully, the sheriff made it out to the ranch and has started the investigation."

Pierce's jaw clenched at the mention of the sheriff.

Cold slithered across Roxanne's skin, reminding her of what she'd been searching for in the first place. She inched her way to the darkest corner, hoping any critters who might have called this cave home had scurried out, preferring the warmth of the summer prairie to the cool darkness. She found the stash of tinder and dry wood they'd left well before her brother's death, still hidden behind a boulder.

As she emerged into the meager light carrying an armful of firewood, Pierce had pulled out the bag of sandwiches and trail mix his mother had insisted on him bringing. When he saw what Roxanne held, he dropped the bag next to the stone ring and relieved her of her burden. "You shouldn't be carrying that. You might get that gash bleeding again."

She thought about arguing but decided it wasn't

worth it. Besides, her arm really did hurt. If he wanted to take care of the fire himself, that was fine with her.

Within minutes a cheerful fire burned brightly, lighting even the darkest corners of the cavern, chasing away the shadows and spiders.

Roxanne laid her saddle blanket on the ground beside the flames to dry, and then collapsed in the dirt close to the fire, grateful for the warmth as the chill of damp clothing set in. Her teeth clattered together, the ache in the back of her head intensifying as the painkiller she'd taken earlier wore off. She rubbed the knot at the base of her skull, kneading the soreness, hoping to ease the ache in the absence of medication.

"Here, let me," said a brusque voice from behind her, and her fingers were brushed aside.

Warm, callused hands curled around her neck. Thumbs avoided the lump, smoothing the hair and skin in gentle circles.

Tense muscles relaxed, the soreness fading as Roxanne pushed aside the fact that Pierce was the source of her relief. For a moment, she let the heat of his fingers chase away the chill inside, leaning back into his broad chest.

The thumbs stilled, and his hands froze against her skin.

A shiver, originating at the base of her spine,

rocketed all the way up her back, shaking her violently. Once the trembling began, it didn't abate.

His hands jerked away from her and he stood, backing up several steps. "You have to get out of those wet clothes."

"And w-what am I s-supposed to wear in the m-mean time?" she quipped, the chattering of her teeth taking the barb out of her response.

"Wearing nothing is better than keeping the dampness against your skin. The moisture conducts heat away from your body."

"I know that." Still, she couldn't quite stomach the thought of undressing in front of him. With everything that had happened with the shooter and her injury, she felt too vulnerable. Common sense told her that she needed to get the clothes away from her skin, but every instinct protested. She couldn't let herself be weak where Pierce Thunder Horse was concerned, lest it create a leak in the dam of emotions she'd held in check since he'd returned.

Stubbornly, she wrapped her arms around her knees, pulling them up against her body for more warmth. Her body's trembles turned into bone-shaking shivers, so violent she thought she'd rattle apart.

"Good grief, woman. It's not as though I haven't seen you naked before." He grabbed her hand and urged her to her feet, standing her in front of him.

His hands clamped down on her shoulders and he rubbed them through the damp cotton of the T-shirt she wore.

"You're freezing. I suspect shock is setting in from your fall and injury. If we don't get you warmed up, you could have some serious problems, and we both know that there's no way I could get you some help until the weather clears."

"Well, when you put it that way." She pressed her hands into his chest, pushing against him. "I can undress myself."

He let go of her, his lips twisting. "Go for it."

Her fingers fumbled with the hem of her shirt. They shook so hard, she couldn't manage to pull it up over her torso. "I don't know…what's… wrong…" Tears welled in her eyes, and before she could stop them, ran down her cheeks. Now she couldn't even see what she was doing.

"Give it up." Pierce's whispered words stirred the wisps of hair beside Roxanne's ear, his breath warming her cold skin.

"Never," she said, though her hands fell to her sides. Giving it up would have to mean trusting him, and she couldn't do that. She *couldn't!* But when he reached out to her again, she found that she couldn't quite bring herself to stop him, either. She'd been cold for so very long…and Pierce was always so warm.

Deft fingers made quick work of tugging her

shirt up and over her head, easing it past the wound on her shoulder and the back of her scalp.

Roxanne's breath lodged in her throat and her gaze traveled upward to connect with the darkness of the Lakotan's eyes. Months of sorrow, of love lost and families betrayed couldn't begin to melt away in one look.

She wanted to say *no,* wanted to shake her head, push him away, stay strong all on her own, the way she had for months. But God help her, she also wanted to say *yes,* to relax and let someone else take control, maybe even take care of her for a little while.

In the end, she didn't say anything at all. Neither did he. Instead, his lips lowered, so slowly she had plenty of time to resist, to turn away and run.

But she didn't.

EVERY THOUGHT, NERVE, beat of Pierce's heart centered on Roxanne. Her fiery red hair lay wet and curling against her face, her mouth opened, her tongue flicking out to slide across her lips.

He bent to capture her full bottom lip between his teeth, sucking it into his mouth.

The lace of Roxanne's bra rubbed against his shirt. The urge to rip aside the fabric swelled inside him. He had to touch the full, rounded softness of her breasts, to smooth his hands over the swells, rediscovering the curves and warmth of Roxanne's naked skin.

He buried his face in the curve of her neck, nipping and sucking at the pulse beating wildly there.

When Pierce realized she was just as affected by him as he was her, he continued his assault, tossing her shirt to the floor. He unclasped her bra, easing the straps over her shoulders and down her arms, his gaze following its progress as her breasts sprang free. He cupped one in his palm and touched the rigid nipple with the tip of his tongue, lost in the taste of her.

Her chest rose on a gasp, her head falling back. Roxanne's hand reached out to circle Pierce's neck, bringing him closer so that he could suck the nipple into his mouth, pulling hard.

Her other hand groped for the top button of his jeans, fumbling with the hard metal rivet. His head rose and he stared down into her smoky blue gaze, seeing the woman he'd fallen in love with, the woman who was his equal, his soul mate, the only one for him. He pulled her hard against his chest and held her, giving in to the way it felt to have her back in his arms. He wanted her so badly his entire body shook with his need.

He had difficulty forcing his thoughts beyond the moment. If he followed his base instincts, he'd throw caution to the wind and take her there, in the darkness of the cave, their naked bodies writhing in the firelight.

But if he did that, she'd never forgive him. When they both came to their senses, Roxanne would remember all the reasons she had to despise him, all the reasons they would never be a couple again, never have a future together.

Pierce dragged in a deep breath and let it out, loosening his hold on her.

This was Roxanne. The woman he still loved with all his heart. The sister of one of the men whose death was his fault.

Pierce couldn't change the past or undo what had happened to Roxanne's brother. He couldn't stop her hating him and hadn't been able to keep her from leaving; nor had he tried. Today was the first time they'd managed to even have a conversation since ending their engagement, and it had been more than enough to show him how angry she still was. Right now, she was cold, and scared, and hurting and she was willing to let his touch make the world go away for a while, but it wouldn't last. Making love to her wouldn't change anything. She still hated him and no matter how perfect she'd been for him, Special Agent Pierce Thunder Horse was the wrong man for her.

He tugged her bra straps up over her shoulders and eased them both down to sit near the campfire, holding her close to share his body warmth.

"That shouldn't have happened," she said, her voice not much louder than a whisper.

"No. It shouldn't have." He didn't try to kiss her again.

She leaned her head against his chest. "It won't happen again."

"Count on it." He held her into the night as she fell into a troubled sleep. She clung to him, her body shaking, her head twisting back and forth as nightmares disturbed her slumber. Because of her possible concussion, he had an excuse to wake her from her dreams every two hours.

In the small hours of the morning, Pierce spooned her body against his, his gaze on the dying embers of the fire, his thoughts swirling around the shooting, the dirt bike, Roxanne and the bullet and wrapper they'd found in the cave.

Sleep escaped him with her body close to his and the wad of evidence in his pocket. The more he mulled over everything, the more dread filled his chest, crushing him with worry.

Whatever Roxanne had stumbled on that had caused the shooter to attack, it was much bigger than some idiot taking potshots at wild horses.

If he wasn't mistaken, the piece of plastic and the claylike substance clinging to it wasn't a candy wrapper for gum, but the packaging used around plastic explosives.

Chapter Four

A horse nickered, stirring Roxanne awake. Her eyes blinked open to the muted light of predawn filtering through the window. Only it wasn't a window, and the cool air brushing across her skin wasn't coming from outside her house.

Her back was warm. An arm draped around her middle and the solid mass pressing against her generated enough heat to chase away the chills, keeping her from freezing in the cool morning air.

Then it all came back to her and she jerked to an upright position, her hands covering her breasts. She breathed a sigh of relief when her hands connected with her bra.

Pierce Thunder Horse pushed up on one elbow, a wary expression on his face. "Morning. Sleep well?"

"Fine." She leaped to her feet, snatching up her T-shirt and jeans. Turning her back to the Lakotan, she jammed her feet into the jeans and shivered as she shimmied the cold but dry fabric up her legs. Thank goodness her shirt and jeans had dried in the night, or moving about in the cool North Dakota morning air would be very uncomfortable. She finger-combed her hair to smooth the curls before she felt confident enough to face Pierce.

Good Lord, what had she done? She'd almost made love to this man.

Without looking him in the eye, she faced Pierce.

He'd pulled his denim shirt over broad shoulders, leaving it hanging open, exposing his smooth, dark chest.

Roxanne realized too late that staring at his chest was every bit as dangerous as looking into his eyes.

"I need to get back to my ranch." The sooner she got away from Pierce, the better.

Pierce frowned as he buttoned his shirt. "It's not safe to go there without an escort. And I'll need to go with you, anyway, in order to bring Sassy back with me." She started to protest, but his jaw tightened and he held up a hand. "Give it up, Roxanne, I'm not taking no for an answer. You're still in danger, and I'm not going to let you ride around this area by yourself."

Roxanne fought the urge to scream in frustration. She couldn't deny that he was right about the danger of riding alone, but she hated to think that she was dependent on him, that she needed his help or protection. She'd spent the past two months convincing herself that she was fine on her own, that she didn't need Pierce or anyone else. Then on the very day that he rode back into her life, she found herself forced to rely on him. And worse, in spite of all her strong, fervent resolutions, she'd even ended up falling back into his arms.

"Just because we…"

"Almost made love?"

"Just because we almost had sex," she corrected him firmly, "doesn't change anything between us. It was a mistake that will never happen again."

Pierce nodded slowly, his dark eyes black and intense. He looked as hurt and tormented as she felt, and in spite of all her anger and pain, part of her still longed to reach out to him, to comfort him and be comforted in return. But that wasn't possible.

"I know," he said, and walked away.

THEY EMERGED FROM THE cave cautiously, Pierce leading the strange little group of humans and horses. Roxanne blinked in the sunlight, her eyes adjusting from the shadows.

Cetan whinnied, shifting from side to side at the end of his lead.

The colt twisted and reared, tugging at the end of the rope Pierce used to lead her out.

A quick scan of the canyon floor revealed the presence of the herd of wild horses. Separating herself from the rest, Sweet Jessie trotted toward them.

Roxanne studied the way the mare moved. "She appears to be all right."

"I can see where she was hit. She has a streak of blood on her right shoulder. But it doesn't seem to bother her."

Roxanne chewed on her bottom lip. "I'd like to inspect her more closely, but I'm afraid capturing her might cause further injury."

The colt pulled hard against the lead, squealing in a high-pitched cry for her mother.

"We'll keep an eye on her."

"*I'll* keep an eye on her," Roxanne replied. "It's not like you'll be around once the wedding is over, anyway. You'll be back to your FBI work."

There was a pause as Pierce seemed to be wrestling over what to say. The foal took the decision out of his hands as she struggled against the rope until Pierce could barely maintain his grip. "In the meantime, this little one wants her mama. I can hold her, if you can loosen the buckle on the halter." He held the frightened animal steady.

Roxanne slipped the straps free of the buckle and slid the halter over the filly's head, her fingers brushing against Pierce's arm.

As soon as the filly was free, Pierce let go. Without pause, the colt bolted for her mother, tossing her head as if in defiance of her time held in captivity.

Sweet Jessie met her halfway, sniffing, nuzzling and herding her errant baby toward the herd.

On a rise a hundred yards from where Pierce and Roxanne stood, the herd stallion rose up on his hind legs, calling out to the mares.

Cetan snorted, his eyes rolling back. He tugged on the reins Roxanne held.

Pierce relieved her of her hold, his hand rising to stroke his stallion's neck, speaking to the animal in his native tongue.

"Come on," Pierce said, his voice low, insistent. "We could do without a fight between stallions."

Roxanne gathered Sassy's reins, placed her foot into the stirrup and swung up into the saddle, her shoulder stiff from her wound and a night sleeping on the hard floor of the cave. She headed for the trail leading out of the canyon, without looking back over her shoulder at Pierce.

The work they'd done to help the filly had been challenging and worthwhile, seeing the colt reunited with her mother. But now that it was done, all of Roxanne's other worries came crashing back in. The shooter who might still be after her. The financial problems she was facing at her ranch. And most troubling of all, the feelings she had for Pierce Thunder Horse that refused to die down.

That didn't make Pierce any less guilty of talking her brother into joining the FBI, or sending him into the situation that eventually got him killed.

Roxanne pushed the past to the back of her mind, the dangerous trail her more immediate concern. She let Sassy choose her footing on the way up.

She waited long enough to ensure Pierce made it out of the canyon. Thankfully, the shooter wasn't watching for them. Neither were the other Thunder Horse men. Based on the angle of the sun hovering over the horizon, it was very early in the morning.

If she was lucky, she could get in a good day's work, despite having lost the day before to the attack. The cattle auction was coming up soon and she had to have her animals loaded and shipped before that day or she'd be in even worse shape financially than she was physically. The thought of the shooter still disturbed her, but it wasn't as if she could go into hiding. She had a ranch to run.

As Pierce and Cetan cleared the rim, Roxanne

nudged Sassy into a canter, headed toward the Carmichael Ranch. She could hear Pierce and Cetan behind her, but didn't rein in to wait for them. She was in too much of a hurry to get home. Having been out of contact for over half a day, she wondered if anything else had gone wrong while she'd been gone.

Thirty minutes later, she rode into the barnyard and dismounted.

Before Pierce could climb down off his horse, Roxanne handed over Sassy's reins. "Thank you for the use of your horse. You can go now."

Pierce's lips quirked at the corners for a moment, but he quickly grew serious again. "You can't dismiss me that easily. What happened with the shooter could happen again."

"Yes, it could. But you sticking around won't change that. He didn't hesitate to shoot at me in front of you before."

Pierce hesitated, his eyes narrowing.

"I have four ranch hands and a foreman running around the place. If that man comes back, he'll definitely be outnumbered. I'll be okay. You can leave now."

Pierce didn't budge.

"Fine," Roxanne said. "I'll make sure I don't ride alone and I'll carry my own rifle." She planted her fists on her hips. "Satisfied?" She shook her head. "You'd think I didn't have a mind of my own."

"The man who attacked you didn't give up easily. He might come back to finish the job."

"Let me worry about that." She dropped her hands to her sides. "Now, if you'll excuse me, I have a ton of work to do, and I want to get it done before I head back out to check on Sweet Jessie." Roxanne strode toward the barn.

Nothing moved behind her, leaving her in no doubt that Pierce wasn't heading home yet.

"My brothers and I will ride out this afternoon and check on Sweet Jessie and the herd," Pierce called out. "No need for you to do it."

Roxanne halted just outside the barn door and faced him, squinting up at him in the morning sunlight. "It's my responsibility. I'll do the checking."

"And we'll be there to help. Three o'clock this afternoon. Don't go out there until then." He waited for her response, glaring down at her.

"Three o'clock." She turned to enter the barn, her gaze avoiding his. She'd go earlier, just to avoid the man.

Pierce's voice carried to her in one last attempt, "Maybe I should stay."

Her head poked out the door, her brows furrowing. "No." With that final response, she entered the barn, refusing to go back out.

She waited for her eyes to adjust to the dim lighting inside the barn and for the sound of re-treating hoofbeats to indicate the barnyard was clear of Pierce Thunder Horse.

As the interior of the barn came into focus, she gasped, her heart fluttering against her ribs.

Across the walls and doors, slashes of red spray paint marred the otherwise clean surfaces.

"STAY OUT OF THE CANYON!"

WITH SASSY'S LEAD ROPE tied to his saddle horn, Pierce headed toward home, reminding himself he was no longer a part of Roxanne's life. The fact that they'd come very close to making love had changed nothing—at least, it didn't seem to have changed anything for Roxanne. It was a dif-ferent story for him. Having her in his arms again had only lengthened the time it would take to get over her. But he *would* get over her. There wasn't any other option.

Pierce knew now that they weren't meant to be together. Not just because they would both always blame Pierce for her brother's death, but also be-cause, with Mason's death, Roxanne was the only Carmichael left. The woman needed a man who'd be around to help her manage the huge Carmi-chael Ranch. Not some adrenaline-junkie spe-cial agent who'd only drop in long enough to get her pregnant before he left on his next mission.

And she didn't need the worry of waiting by the phone for the call that would inform her that yet another member of her family had given his life for his country. No. Roxanne deserved a better man than Pierce Thunder Horse. Even if she did forgive him for her brother's death, he couldn't add to her heartache by being an absentee husband and father.

The image of her lying near-naked in his arms on the floor of the cave flashed through his mind, weakening his conviction. He wanted to hold her again.

His jaw tightened, along with his resolve. Pierce Thunder Horse would have to get over Roxanne Carmichael. For her own good, if not his own.

As he rode into the Thunder Horse barnyard, his brothers streamed out of the barn, carrying bridles and horse blankets, in the middle of saddling their horses.

Maddox met him first, taking Sassy's reins. "Did you run across the shooter?"

Dante held Cetan's head as Pierce dismounted. "Where's the filly?" he asked.

"More important, where's Roxanne?" Tuck asked, bringing up the rear.

"No more encounters with the shooter, the filly was reunited with Sweet Jessie, Sweet Jessie is wounded but holding her own, and Roxanne insisted on returning to her ranch."

"How was it, spending the night in a cave with your ex?" Dante chuckled. "Prickly?"

Yes, and also very much no. Pierce tipped his head down, hoping the shadow of his cowboy hat would hide any expression on his face. "We made do." He dropped to the ground and led Cetan into the barn. "What did you hear from the sheriff on the bullet casings?"

"Nothing."

Pierce dug in his pocket for the bullet and plastic wrapper, unfolding the wad of cloth surrounding the items. "I take it you kept one of the casings?"

"I did." Tuck's lip curled upward on one side. "Whatcha got there?"

Pierce handed him the wadding. "Get the casing and this bullet and plastic wrapper to the state crime lab, personally. Have them check for a match between the two and see if they can lift prints or even partial prints on any of it."

"Got it." Tuck unfolded the cloth and stared down at the bullet. "Looks close if not exact on the casing. Is this what I suspect it is?"

Pierce's gut clenched. "The wrapper usually found around plastic explosives? Yeah."

Maddox whistled. "Where did you find it?"

"In the cave. Seems our shooter has been camping out on Carmichael property." His fists tightened at the thought that Roxanne wasn't safe on her own spread.

He loosened the girth around Cetan's middle and slipped the saddle over his back. "What I don't understand is why someone would target Roxanne."

Dante replaced Cetan's bridle with a halter and tossed a brush to Tuck, who started running it across the animal's back. "I can't figure that one out at all," Dante said. "The Carmichaels have been a part of this community for a long time. As far as I know, they have no enemies."

"For some reason, Roxanne does now." Pierce hefted the saddle onto a saddletree in the tack room and hung the bridle on a hook. "And she doesn't seem to understand how serious the situation is."

Tuck grinned. "You, of all people, know she's not going to let a little thing like being shot at slow her down. When she sets her mind to getting something done, hell better get out of her way."

Pierce nodded. He remembered.

The woman was as hardheaded as any one of the Thunder Horse brothers. She had to be, in order to run a ranch on her own after her father's death. Even when her brother had been alive, she'd been the one to manage the daily up-keep and operations, while Mason followed his own dreams of being an FBI special agent.

Pierce remembered how excited Mason had been when he'd started his FBI training. Despite Roxanne's belief to the contrary, Pierce had tried to talk Mason out of joining the FBI, telling him that he needed to help his sister with ranch operations. But Mason had that Carmichael stubbornness, too, and in the end, Pierce hadn't been able to change his mind. At the time, he'd consoled himself with the thought that he would always be there, both to help Roxanne with the ranch and to keep an eye on Mason. Now, he couldn't do either.

Pierce shook his head, pushing the thoughts away. That was the past. The present held more pressing matters. With a currycomb, Pierce tackled Cetan's other side. "Did the sheriff ever go out to the site of the shooting?"

Tuck shook his head. "No."

Pierce snorted. "Didn't expect he would."

"Seemed satisfied with the bullet casing. Like it would catch the culprit."

"The man's a waste of the badge he wears," Dante said.

"Came out, flirted with Mom and left," Maddox added. "Seemed like he couldn't have cared less about the shooting, taking the opportunity to investigate as an open door to our mother."

Tuck stuffed the wad of fabric containing the bullet into his jeans pocket. "He did say he'd go to the Carmichael place and ask Roxanne a few questions today."

Pierce's teeth ground together. He'd like to be there when the sheriff stopped by Roxanne's. The lawman would be more hassle than help.

Again, he had to remind himself Roxanne Carmichael would no longer accept his help.

"Julia's worried about Roxanne." Tuck's words interrupted Pierce's thoughts. "Do you suppose one of us should camp out at the Carmichael ranch until they find this guy?"

"She wouldn't let us if we tried."

Tuck grinned. "I know. Just thought I'd suggest it. It would make Julia happier."

"You two have your own worries, what with the wedding coming up fast. How many days now?"

"Five." Finished on his side, Tuck rounded the horse's backside and collected the currycomb from Pierce. "But if things get worse with that shooter, we might have to postpone."

"No way. You two deserve each other."

Tuck laughed. "I'll take that as a compliment." His smile straightened and he clapped a hand on Pierce's shoulder, leaning in to speak so that only Pierce could hear. "Look, Pierce, I know this was supposed to be your time. You should have been married by now, not me. I just wanted you to know, I'm here for you if you need to talk."

"About what?" Pierce stepped away from his brother, letting Tuck's hand fall to his side. The last thing he needed was his brother's pity.

"You could talk about Roxanne, the wedding..." He shrugged. "You know...things."

Pierce took the brush and currycomb back from Tuck's hand. "I've got nothing to say. Our breakup is old history. I'm over her."

Tuck hesitated for a moment, as if he wanted to say more. Then he nodded. "The offer is open. Whenever you need me, I'm here to listen." He didn't wait for a response, instead leaving the barn. Maddox and Dante followed him shortly after.

Pierce stood with the brush in his hand, his chest squeezing so tight he couldn't breathe. If he was so over Roxanne, why did he feel like he was having a heart attack?

He forced himself to go through the motions of brushing Cetan from front to rear, one more time. His hands moved slowly, one steadying stroke at a time until they quit shaking and he could breathe normally.

All the while, he pictured Roxanne lying next to him on the cave floor, her pale white skin almost glowing in the darkness, her soft curves nestled against him.

Yeah, he was over her.

Chapter Five

Roxanne called the sheriff's office as soon as she'd discovered the paint in the barn.

Deputy Shorty Duncan showed up in less than an hour to question her on the events of the day before and to take pictures of the damage done in the barn.

He spent time with each of her ranch hands, questioning them about their whereabouts during the night, but nothing came of it. According to their accounts, no one had seen anything and Roxanne hadn't been there to verify.

As he slipped the pad he'd been taking notes on into his pocket, the deputy faced Roxanne. "I've got what I need."

"Any idea who would do this or why they'd want me to stay out of the canyon?"

Duncan shook his head. "No, ma'am, but I'll be checking into it. You can be sure of that." He tucked his pen in with the pad. "In the meantime,

I suggest you stay out of the canyon. Sounds like trouble."

"Aren't you going to check out the canyon to see why someone would want me to stay out?"

"Soon as I get some backup to go with me, I sure will. Don't you worry."

"Not much help, was he?" Jim Rausch, her ranch foreman, said as he stepped up beside her to watch the deputy drive away.

"Wonder when he plans to be back out to check the canyon?"

"No tellin'."

Roxanne sighed. "We can't wait for the law— we have cattle to round up. We'll save the canyon for last."

Jim nodded toward the hands gathered with their horses and called out, "We're burnin' daylight. Mount up."

Roxanne spent the rest of the morning and part of the afternoon with her ranch hands, mending the fences and loading chutes, preparing for the roundup. It made no sense to herd the cattle into the corrals until all the preparatory work had been taken care of. And maybe the routine mending would give the sheriff and his men time to check out the canyon.

Two of the hands worked a downed fence on the northern perimeter, while the other two worked the fences in the holding pens.

Roxanne and her foreman removed and replaced weathered boards on the loading chute.

She'd worked through lunch while her men had stopped for sandwiches, preferring the solitude to sustenance. She couldn't have eaten had she wanted to, her stomach remaining knotted since Pierce had left.

The work was slow and steady…and very tiring. As two o'clock rolled around, she strode over to her foreman. She hated to slow down the work by taking him away from his duties, but after being shot at the day before, she knew she couldn't risk riding out alone, especially to the canyon. Despite Pierce's promise to check on the horses along with his brothers, she knew she needed to see for herself that the herd hadn't been harmed. And for her own peace of mind, she wanted to see to that *without* Pierce beside her.

"I need you to ride over to the canyon with me to check on Sweet Jessie."

"Sure you want to do that, Miss Carmichael?"

"I need to make sure Sweet Jessie and the rest of the herd are okay."

Jim gathered his reins and turned his horse, glancing down at his watch. "Didn't Mr. Pierce say to meet them out there at three o'clock?"

"And we will. But I wanted to get a jump on finding Sweet Jessie to save them some time and the possibility of trouble in the canyon," she lied.

She really wanted to get out there, find Sweet Jessie and get back to her ranch without spending any more time than she had to in the presence of the Thunder Horses, one in particular.

"I'd feel better with them there." He pushed his hat back on his head and stared to the north. "There's safety in numbers."

"We'll be fine, with you as my backup. There was only one shooter."

"Still not likin' it, but if it's what you want, let's get a move on. There's still lots to be done out here."

Jim and Roxanne saddled up and headed out across the prairie.

Roxanne clamped her cowboy hat down on her head, glad for the shade as the sun beat down on her shoulders. The heat of summer had settled into the badlands of North Dakota. Without a tree in sight, the land baked, waves of heat radiating from the dry earth, making the early-morning chill a dim memory.

A trickle of sweat slipped down between Roxanne's breasts and she shifted in her saddle, her jeans clinging to her damp legs.

Roxanne slowed her paint horse to a walk. The heat would tire the horses faster than the speed and she wanted to conserve energy for their return.

Jim rode up alongside her and settled into the

slower, steadier pace. After a while, he glanced over at her. "You know, Pierce is a good man."

At the mention of Pierce's name, Roxanne's heartbeat kicked up a notch. "Can we talk about something else?"

Jim shrugged. "Just saying." He rode in silence for a few more minutes.

Roxanne breathed easier after a while, certain Jim wasn't going to continue selling Pierce.

Then he cleared his throat and said, "You two had somethin' special. You don't find that often, you know."

She glared at her foreman. "I don't want to discuss the man. Besides, you're one to talk. Since when are you an expert on relationships?"

Again, the older man shrugged. "I was in love once."

Roxanne's brows rose. "I didn't know that. I've never even seen you with a woman."

He frowned. "I go to town on my days off. Not that it's any of yer business, little girl."

She smiled, glad they weren't talking about her and Pierce anymore. "I'm not so little anymore."

"My point exactly. You're getting older and need to settle down while you're still breedin' age."

"Jim Rausch, you make me sound like a broodmare." She shook her head. "I don't want to settle with or for anyone. Not now or anytime soon. I'm doing just fine on my own." It was mostly true. She'd *make* it true. Just as soon as she convinced her silly heart not to pine for Pierce.

"You ought to reconsider your opinion of that Thunder Horse boy. He's still pretty stuck on you."

"Don't go there. You know he's the reason Mason joined the FBI, and that it's his fault Mason got himself killed."

"Not the way I see it." Jim rode in silence for a long second or two, before adding, "Mason had his own reasons for joining the FBI. You can't blame it on Pierce."

"Pierce sent him into that building that blew up."

"Now how was he supposed to know the building would explode?"

The image of a fiery explosion had haunted her dreams and memories for months. Roxanne didn't need a reminder. "I'm the wrong one to ask. I don't know the details, and Pierce refused to tell me." *Even when I begged him to explain, to tell me what had happened.* "All he'd say was that Mason's death was his fault. I'm not marrying Pierce Thunder Horse and nothing you can say will change my mind."

"A woman's got a way of changing her own mind."

"Don't hold your breath." She nudged her horse

to go a little faster, trying to put distance between her and Jim.

Unfortunately, he remained abreast. Jim glanced at her, his lips curled ever so slightly. "Just saying."

Roxanne clamped her lips shut, refusing to further the conversation by replying to him.

As they neared the canyon's rim, she slowed her horse, her gaze darting right and left. As far as she could see, nothing moved across the edge. That didn't mean a shooter wasn't lurking, but for now, Roxanne felt confident they were alone on the plains. She patted the rifle protruding from the scabbard on her saddle. Between her and Jim, it was two against one, and they were both armed. That ought to keep the attacker from making a move.

"I'll go down first. When I'm close to the bottom of the trail, you can start down. In the meantime, keep your rifle ready."

"I got yer back, Miss Carmichael." Jim pulled his weapon out and checked the chamber.

She smiled at the man she'd known for as long as she could remember. "Thanks, Jim. When I get to the bottom, I'll cover for you."

Domino, her black-and-white paint gelding, wasn't too keen on the narrow trail. After a little gentle persuasion, Roxanne got him headed in the right direction.

He picked his way down the steep trail, his

steps slow and nervous. At several particularly dangerous points, pebbles slipped over the side and tumbled to the bottom.

Domino tossed his black mane and nickered, his eyes rolling back.

Roxanne smoothed her hand across his long, sleek neck. "Easy, boy. Just a little farther."

Ten feet from the bottom, she pulled the rifle from her scabbard and waved it up at Jim.

The foreman began his descent more easily. His horse was older, more docile and sure-footed.

Roxanne twisted in her saddle, careful to check all directions for a possible threat.

When Jim and his bay mare hit the halfway point, the hair on Roxanne's arm stood on end and she glanced over her shoulder. Nothing. She turned in her saddle to get a better look behind her.

A movement along the canyon rim caught her attention, and Roxanne's heart stopped. Someone was up there.

A jumble of rocks and boulders tumbled down the hill toward Jim and his horse, kicking up dust and more rocks in its path.

"Get out of the way!" Jim shouted, urging his horse to hurry in an attempt to beat the landslide.

Domino reared and backed away from the base of the trail, whinnying wildly.

With one hand holding the rifle, Roxanne

struggled to keep her seat and maintain control of her gelding.

The rattle of rocks grew to a roar as a large boulder bumped down the steep slope.

Roxanne's breath caught in her lungs and she froze.

Jim and his horse were directly in the boulder's path.

"Move!" she shouted, waving the hand holding the rifle. "Move!"

Jim glanced behind him, his eyes rounding. He dug his heels into the horse's flank, startling the horse.

The mare leaped forward and reared as the boulder passed by, narrowly missing them both. The mare recovered her footing, but Jim lost his seat and tumbled out of the saddle.

As if in slow motion, he landed on the downhill side of the trail, bouncing off the rocky slope and cartwheeling downward, picking up speed with the landslide of rocks and gravel.

The foreman somersaulted, slid and bounced the rest of the way down the five-hundred-foot drop, landing in a rush of stones and gravel with a sickening thud.

Roxanne dug her heels into Domino's sides and raced to the base of the slope, her heart hammering against her ribs so hard it hurt.

"Jim. Oh, dear God, Jim," she cried as she

dropped to the ground and crouched over the older man's still form.

Pebbles and small rocks continued to slide down, pelting her face and arms, some of them sharp, drawing blood.

Roxanne didn't care. Jim was her only family, the man who'd been a father to her when her own had died.

"Jim." She reached for the base of his throat and pressed two fingers to his skin, praying with all her heart for a pulse.

"Please be alive. Please."

She held her breath, willing her shaking hands to steady. Finally a faint pulse bumped against her fingertips and she let out a long shaky sigh. "Thank God."

But when she took stock of his form, her vision blurred and she sat back hard on her heels.

Jim lay at an awkward angle, his ankle twisted beneath a rock, his face pale, scratches bleeding across every exposed surface. And never once did he open his eyes.

Roxanne raised her face to the sky and cried, "Help! Please, oh please, help!"

"SITTIN' LIGHT IN THE saddle today, brother?" Dante settled his cowboy hat on his head, pushing it down tight as he swung up on his black gelding.

Pierce eased himself into his own saddle on Cetan. "I got saddle sores from riding the past two days."

"Need to rebuild the calluses on your butt, brother. Becoming a softy in the agent business," Maddox teased. "I'll take the truck with the medical supplies."

"Says the man who rides horses for a living," Pierce quipped.

"I'll let you two do all the fun stuff in the canyon while I provide cover from above. Besides, someone's got to haul the medical supplies in case Sweet Jessie needs them, and they ain't gonna fit on the back of your horse."

"Yeah, yeah. You'll be napping, old man." Dante clicked his tongue and his horse trotted out of the barnyard.

Maddox caught Pierce's gaze, all kidding wiped from his face. "Nothing from Tuck, yet?"

"Nothing more than what you already know. The bullet and casings are a match. He couldn't lift any prints. He's trying to get a trace on the plastic explosives, but there wasn't much to go on."

Maddox nodded. "You two will catch this guy. I know I can count on my FBI brothers to always get their man."

"I just hope we get him before he gets Roxanne."

"Yeah." Maddox's head dipped and he fiddled with the leather gloves he carried. "Speaking of Roxanne…"

Pierce held up a hand. "Don't go there. We're history."

"Spending the night in a cave alone with her didn't stir up any lingering anything?" Maddox gave him a pointed stare.

"We weren't alone. We had three horses in the cave with us."

Maddox snorted. "You're avoiding the question."

"No, I'm not answering it. Come on, we'll be late for our three o'clock with the woman at this rate."

Before he could leave the barnyard, Pierce spied Maddox's fiancée running from the house toward them, carrying a pair of walkie-talkies.

"Maddox, you got company."

The pretty, dark-haired princess of a breakaway Russian nation skidded to a halt, breathing hard. "You almost forgot your radio." After she handed him one, she stood for a moment, staring up at him, the love shining from her eyes. "Be careful, please." Then she flung her arms around his neck and pressed her lips to his.

Maddox's arms circled her tiny waist, pulling her close, deepening the kiss.

Pierce's gut knotted.

Maddox and Katya were so in love it made Pierce want to gag.

He dug his heels into Cetan's flanks, startling the animal into a jerky lope. Pierce didn't slow the horse until he was well out of eyesight of the barn, his brother and his brother's fiancée.

He told himself he was better off single. He'd be no kind of husband to any woman, and especially not to Roxanne.

Tuck was crazy to think a relationship between him and Julia would work out while he stayed an agent, even though Julia had already told Tuck she wouldn't stand in the way of his career, that she wanted him to follow his dream of being an FBI special agent.

He'd end up quitting the FBI in order to stay home with his wife and baby daughter. From what Pierce had seen, Tuck would give up breathing for Lily and Julia, and Pierce had seen the worry in Julia's eyes every time Tuck headed back to the office in Bismarck. She'd worry about him until he returned, even though Tuck was a good agent who'd given her no reason to doubt his ability to come home to her at the end of the day. Not like Pierce, who had already let Roxanne down when his mistake ended in her brother's death.

Even if Roxanne forgave Pierce for Mason's death, he would never forgive himself. Pierce couldn't ask her again to be his wife. Being the cause of her brother's death would always stand between them, not to mention the loneliness, heartache and uncertainty of being the spouse of an agent.

Pierce caught up with Dante and they rode side by side in silence the rest of the way out to the canyon on the border of the Thunder Horse and Carmichael ranches. Dante didn't mention Roxanne and Pierce didn't bring her up, preferring to push on, keeping his thoughts completely to himself.

As they neared the trailhead Pierce and Roxanne had ascended earlier that morning, a slew of emotions rippled across his consciousness, the foremost being regret.

Regret that things hadn't worked out differently, that it had been inevitable they turned out the way they did.

What if Mason had lived? What if he and Roxanne had continued with their wedding plans? They'd be married now.

And their marriage would have been a huge mistake. Roxanne deserved a man she could count on, and that could never be him.

A distant cry echoed off the canyon walls, pushing thoughts of what might have been to the back of Pierce's mind.

"Did you hear that?" Dante asked.

Both men pulled on their reins and listened.

"Help!" The desperate sound rose from somewhere down in the canyon.

Pierce's pulse leaped. "Roxanne?" He slapped his reins on his horse's flanks. Cetan burst into a gallop, heading straight for the trail.

"Pierce, wait!" Dante called out behind him.

At the last moment, Cetan skidded to a halt, sending a shower of pebbles and gravel over the edge.

"Help! Please, help us!" Roxanne's voice called out.

Pierce dropped down off Cetan's back and peered over the rim of the canyon.

Roxanne knelt beside a distorted figure lying among the rocks. When she glanced up, she pointed her rifle up at him and shouted, "Who's there?"

"Roxanne, it's me, Pierce." His voice echoed several times off the walls of the canyon.

"Thank God," Roxanne said, and laid the rifle on the ground, kneeling in the dirt beside the man.

"I'm going down." Pierce handed his reins to his brother.

Dante caught his arm. "Be careful, Pierce. Looks like there's been an avalanche." He nodded toward the edge where a large chunk of the rim had recently fallen away.

Pierce's throat constricted. Roxanne could have

been the one lying hurt at the bottom of the canyon. He left Cetan at the top and walked down the steep trail, his boots slipping on newly loosened stone. At one point the trail all but disappeared, ripped away by a rush of stone and debris.

When he reached the bottom, he hurried across to where Roxanne sat on the ground, holding Jim Rausch's hand, the tears trickling down her face forming long trails through the dust caked to her skin. She glanced up at Pierce. "Don't let him die."

Pierce dropped to his haunches next to Jim's body and felt for a pulse. "He's still with us. How long has he been out?"

"Fifteen, twenty minutes, maybe." She shook her head as she stared at the man. "He fell most of the way down and I couldn't do a thing."

"Moving him could cause more damage. We'll have to get an airlift to get him out of here."

Pierce glanced up to the rim of the canyon. Maddox had arrived and waited beside Dante. Pierce stood and waved at his brothers.

Dante started the long trek down the damaged trail.

"I'll be back." As Pierce turned to go, Roxanne's hand grabbed his leg.

"Hurry." Her voice broke, and another tear slipped down her cheek.

Pierce forced himself to move away, climbing

the trail as fast as he could to meet Dante halfway up.

"Is it Jim?" Dante asked, his gaze moving past Pierce to the man lying so still. "Is he dead?"

"It's Jim and he's still alive. Tell Maddox to radio back to the house and have someone call nine-one-one. We need an emergency medical helicopter here ASAP."

"Got it." Dante turned and scrambled back up the trail.

Pierce returned to the base and Roxanne.

He sat on the ground beside her and gathered her in his arms. "He'll be okay."

She turned her face into his chest, her fingers bunching his shirt. "Promise?"

"I can't promise, but we'll do the best we can."

She didn't reply...but she didn't let go, either.

For the longest time they sat there, waiting for the reassuring thumping of rotor blades beating the air.

When it finally came, Pierce stood, gathered the horses' reins and held them steady as a helicopter hovered over the canyon and then landed on a flat patch of ground on the canyon floor. At the same time, a handful of emergency medical personnel descended from the rim of the canyon, carrying medical supplies and a backboard.

Pierce pulled Roxanne away from Jim, leaving him in the care of the professionals. He stood with her hand clasped in his, his heart aching for her. Pierce knew what Jim meant to Roxanne.

Jim Rausch was more family to Roxanne than employee. Having survived her brother's death, she'd be devastated by the loss of her foreman.

He prayed to the Great Spirit to spare the man's life for Roxanne's sake. She didn't need to go through all that again.

Roxanne broke away from him and followed the medical team as they carried Jim on the backboard to the waiting helicopter.

After they loaded the foreman into the helicopter and it lifted off the ground, the technicians returned to clear their equipment.

Roxanne trudged back, her head down until she reached Pierce. "He has to make it."

"Jim's a tough guy. He'll pull through."

Roxanne's face turned up to his, her normally bright blue eyes nearly gray, shadowed. "I watched him fall all that way down."

Pierce pulled her into his arms. "You couldn't have done a thing to help. It was an accident."

"No it wasn't."

"She's right—it wasn't."

Pierce turned at Maddox's voice.

His brother was stepping off the trail onto the floor of the canyon.

Roxanne straightened. "I know I saw someone,

standing at the ledge right before the avalanche started. Was it him? Did he do this?"

Maddox nodded, his mouth set in a grim line. "You'll want to take a look at this, Pierce. From the tracks he left behind, there's no denying it. Someone forced that boulder free, setting off that avalanche."

Chapter Six

Roxanne paced the corridor of the St. Alexius Medical Center in Bismarck, the acrid scent of rubbing alcohol and disinfectant burning the insides of her nostrils, bringing back nothing but bad memories.

She hated hospitals. Every time she'd gone to one, someone she'd loved had died. Her father, her mother and, more recently, her brother. Now Jim lay in a hospital room—and it was her fault. She should have heeded the warning not to go into the canyon.

Pierce leaned against the wall, his arms crossed. "Getting yourself all worked up won't help Jim."

"I don't need advice, I need answers." She stopped in midstride and glared at Pierce. "Who did this? And why?"

He shook his head. "We don't know. We didn't see any dirt bike tracks this time."

"I didn't hear a motorcycle, but then I was at

the bottom looking up...." She scuffed her boot across the polished tiles. "I should have seen more, enough to identify the bastard."

Pierce grabbed her shoulders and forced her to look at him. "Once you realized what was happening, you kept your eyes on Jim. And from what you said earlier, if you hadn't been watching him, he could have been hit by a boulder traveling at top speed."

Roxanne's body shook with her anger. "This psycho has to be stopped before someone is killed."

"My brothers are searching the canyon rim for more tracks. He couldn't have gone far without a horse or an ATV. If there are tracks, Maddox and Dante will find them."

"Why Jim?" Roxanne asked, her brows drawing together.

"Do you mean, why not you?" Pierce shot back at her. "You can't blame yourself, Roxy."

"I was stupid, I should have heeded the warning."

Pierce frowned. "What warning?"

Roxanne tipped her head back, running her hand through her hair. "When you dropped me off this morning, I went inside the barn and found a message spray painted across the walls."

Pierce shook her slightly. "What did it say?"

"'Stay out of the canyon.'" She broke free of his grip and walked away. "And I didn't."

"Why didn't you call me?"

She spun to face him, anger at herself digging a hole in her gut. "I didn't want you to come back around. It wasn't your problem. I called the sheriff and Deputy Duncan came out, asked questions and said he'd check into it."

Pierce snorted. "You should have called me back before I'd even left."

She flung her hand in the air. "Hindsight isn't doing Jim any good now."

A nurse emerged from Jim's room, pushing a cart of bloody gauze and surgical equipment. She gave Roxanne a reassuring smile. "Dr. Rhoads will be out shortly."

Her stomach knotting, Roxanne quickly settled herself in a chair as she felt her knees start to give way. Her breath caught and held in her throat as she waited for the doctor to appear. A crash cart hadn't been wheeled in. That had to be a good sign. The nurse had smiled. Another good sign.

Jim had to be all right.

She gulped back the sob that threatened to rise in her throat, calling on all the anger that had been simmering to force herself to stay strong and in control.

When the doctor emerged, Roxanne practically pounced on him. "How's Jim? Will he be all right?"

The doctor's brows dipped. "Are you his next of kin?"

"I'm his boss and the only family Jim has. That makes me next of kin." Roxanne stared up at the doctor. "I have power of attorney, but the paperwork is back at the ranch."

"Good enough." Dr. Rhoads nodded and laid a hand on Roxanne's shoulder. "He's pretty banged up, but for a man his age, he's in good physical condition and should pull through just fine."

Roxanne let go of the breath she'd been holding. "Thank God."

"He's got a broken arm, sprained ankle and two broken ribs. Had a helluva time getting his boot off. Ended up cutting it away. Since he took such hard knocks to the head, we'll keep him overnight to make sure he doesn't have any swelling on the brain."

Roxanne's chest tightened at the recurring image of Jim tumbling down the steep walls of the canyon. "He fell a long way."

Dr. Rhoads laid a hand on Roxanne's arm. "We'll keep him in the intensive care unit overnight and check on him every half hour. The good news is that he did recover consciousness while we were patching him up and asked for Miss Roxy. I assume that's you?"

Roxanne's eyes clouded with tears. Jim hadn't called her Roxy since her father had died. "That's me. Can I see him?"

"He's hooked up to monitors and oxygen, but yes, though only for a few minutes. He won't be awake for long, I have the nurse administering a sedative in his IV. It should kick in pretty quickly."

Pierce flipped out his credentials. "I'm with the FBI. If he's awake, I'd like to ask Jim some questions about what happened."

Dr. Rhoads's lips tightened. "Don't take too long. He's been through a lot."

Roxanne shook the doctor's hand. "Thank you so much for taking care of him." Then she scooted around him and into the room, Pierce close behind.

Another nurse was inside, adjusting an IV bag. When she saw them, she smiled and left them alone with the foreman.

Jim lay in the hospital bed, his rugged, sun-baked skin a sharp contrast to the crisp white sheets.

Her chest squeezing tight, Roxanne tiptoed to his bedside and took his work-worn uninjured hand in hers, carefully, afraid she'd hurt him.

Her old friend's eyes blinked open and stared up at her for a long moment. "Watch that first step," he said, his voice like gravel, rough and broken. "It's a doozy." He chuckled and winced.

A tear slipped from the corner of Roxanne's eye. Jim always had a way of making her laugh when times were at their worst. "You never did like following the leader," she said. "You had to go and make a path of your own, didn't you?"

He closed his eyes and whispered, "Faster."

She squeezed his hand, reminded of just how quickly it had happened, even in the slow motion of her traumatized view. "Show-off." Her voice caught on a sob.

Jim's brow furrowed. "Hey, what's this? Cowgirls don't cry."

She brushed a tear away, but more followed. "This one does."

"Go home, Miss Roxy." He squeezed her hand.

"Not without you."

"Gonna be there soon enough."

She smiled, feeling better at the reminder that he wouldn't have to be in the hospital for long. "You better."

"Now go, cowgirl." His voice faded.

For a moment Roxanne thought he'd drifted to sleep. She held on to his hand, afraid that if she let go something bad would happen.

Jim's lids twitched open. "Got my eye on one of the nurses. You're cramping my style."

Pierce touched her shoulder. "Come on, the old man needs his rest."

"And a good-lookin' nurse." Jim glanced up at Roxanne. "I'll be fine. Just need a little nap." He closed his eyes again and his breathing grew slow and steady.

Roxanne laid his hand on the bed and backed away, reluctant to leave.

Pierce hooked her arm and led her through the door.

"I should stay," she said, staring at the closed door.

"And do what? The nurses are going to keep an eye on him all night. It's getting late and we need to get back."

Roxanne knew he was right, but leaving Jim...

"Look, Dante went by your place earlier to let them know what was going on and get a look at that spray paint. I'm sure your ranch hands would appreciate an update."

Roxanne's shoulders sagged as her world rushed back in, reminding her of her responsibilities as a ranch owner. With her foreman out and herself here in Bismarck, there was no telling how the cattle roundup was progressing. She couldn't afford to lose another day or she'd miss the sale and her only opportunity to make enough money to keep the ranch afloat through the winter. At that rate, she'd have to lay off all the hands and she wouldn't have anything to pay the mortgage, the men, Jim or his medical bills. "You're right. I need to get back to the ranch." She spun on her boot heels and headed for the exit.

Since Maddox had brought the truck to the canyon, Pierce and Roxanne had taken it all the way to Bismarck to check on Jim while Dante and Maddox had taken care of getting the horses home. Pierce would have to take her back to her ranch.

Roxanne left the hospital and climbed into the truck cab, sinking back against the seat, letting the worry for Jim's safety roll off her.

She breathed in the earthy scent of hay and leather gloves, remembering the many times she'd ridden in this old truck, worked alongside Pierce as they loaded hay onto trailers, hauling it back to be stored in the barn. The memories reminded her of hot summer days and cool, lazy nights, sitting on the porch of her ranch house, just the two of them in the swing her grandfather had built for her grandmother. The old couple had been married over seventy years when they'd passed on within months of each other.

Roxanne had assumed she and Pierce would be like them, sitting on the porch swing, growing old, celebrating their seventieth year together with their grandchildren gathered around.

She shook her head, sitting up straighter in her

seat, her eyes focusing on the road ahead. She had been mistaken. Their union wasn't meant to be.

After Pierce pulled onto Interstate 94, he glanced across at her.

"You should stay at the Thunder Horse Ranch tonight."

His words ripped through the silence, startling a response out of her. "What?"

"You heard me. Someone has made a point of going after you and your people. It's not safe for you to go back. My brothers and I can protect you better at our place."

"And leave my ranch and the hands at the mercy of some lunatic?" She crossed her arms over her chest. "Thanks, but no thanks."

In her peripheral vision Roxanne could see him staring at her, but she refused to look his way. She'd leaned on him entirely too much that day already. It wasn't as if he'd be there always. He'd told her she couldn't rely on him, and she'd taken him at his word.

In this, as in everything else in her life, she was on her own.

SILENCE SETTLED AROUND them in the cab of the pickup as Pierce accepted that this was one battle he wasn't going to win. He knew that Roxanne couldn't leave her ranch hands to fend for themselves. Much as he'd like to spirit her away from it all to keep her safe, her sense of responsibility wouldn't let her go.

The warning message led him to believe the canyon was the only place the shooter had issues with, so perhaps she was safe as long as she stayed on the ranch. But the message had appeared inside her barn, close to her home. Pierce didn't trust that the attacker wouldn't make it more personal. How could he keep her safe?

The rumble of tires on the road vibrated through his chest. The thought of Roxanne staying on her ranch without the foreman ate a hole in Pierce's gut.

Jim was the oldest and most trusted employee she had and he'd stayed in the ranch house since the deaths of Roxanne's parents. With Jim out of the way, someone might take advantage of the opportunity and make a move on Roxanne, a lone woman in an empty house.

By the time he pulled onto the long gravel driveway leading up to the Carmichael ranch house, he'd made up his mind.

Now all he had to do was convince Roxanne.

He shifted into Park in front of her house.

She glanced sideways at him. "Thanks for taking me to Bismarck."

"I'd have gone anyway." Pierce switched off the engine. "I wanted to see that Jim was okay. He's a good man."

When Roxanne opened her door and climbed down, Pierce did the same.

She stared across the cab of the truck at him, without closing the door. "I can take it from here. You don't have to stick around."

"I'm staying." He closed the driver's door.

"Oh, no, you're not." She slammed her door and rounded the front of his truck, grabbed his door handle and opened it again. "Tuck needs you to help him with wedding planning."

Pierce shut the door again. "I'm staying."

"I don't need you to. I have four ranch hands as backup."

"And they stay in the bunkhouse while you are alone in the main house." He crossed his arms over his chest and stared down at her, feet braced, ready for the fight. "I'm staying."

She frowned. "You're not welcome, so go home."

"You need protection. I'm it."

"I have a gun. I'll provide my own protection." She jerked her hand toward the truck. "Go."

He shook his head, his lip lifting on one side. "Sorry. No can do. You're stuck with me."

"You're not staying in the ranch house." She heaved a sigh, her shoulders sagging, the shadows beneath her eyes deepening. "Please leave."

"Not going to happen. Look, if you don't want me in the house then I'll sleep outside." He raised his hands above his head and stretched. "Been a few years since I slept under the stars. Reckon it will be good for me."

She dragged in a breath and blew it out through her nose like an angry bull. "You're a stubborn man, Pierce Thunder Horse."

"I can be."

"Fine. If you're staying, it has to be in the bunkhouse with the hands."

"Kind of missing the point, aren't you? I won't be close enough to help you if someone tries to come after you."

"That's as good as it gets, cowboy."

Pierce's eyes narrowed. At least she wasn't booting him off her property or calling the sheriff to have him removed. "Done."

He opened the rear door to the cab and unearthed a sleeping bag he kept rolled up behind the seat in case of a breakdown. Being prepared meant the difference between life and death during the North Dakota winters. Granted it was summer, but the bag remained in the truck year-round, just in case.

Roxanne turned toward the house, her voice carrying over her shoulder. "I'll fix a sandwich for you. I'm sure the hands have already rustled up their grub. Give me twenty minutes."

He nodded and took off toward the bunkhouse. He still didn't plan to sleep there—the distance to the house was too much for his comfort. However, it was his chance to check out Roxanne's employees. One of them could be the trouble-maker.

As he entered the long barracks-style building, four heads turned his way. "Evenin'." He touched the brim of his hat and strode in. "Looks like I'll be helpin' with the roundup. Miss Carmichael said to bunk here."

Pierce nodded at Abe Hunting Bear and Fred Jorgensen, men he'd known as long as he'd known Roxanne.

"We could use the help, Pierce." Abe offered his hand. "Seems the herd is scattered farther than normal this year. The early drought has them ranging wide to get enough to eat."

Pierce braced himself as the Lakotan gripped his hand hard enough to crush bones. When Abe let go, Pierce shook his hand, letting blood rush back in. "Good to see ya, Abe."

Fred proffered a hand, his gaze direct. He didn't utter a single word, just shook Pierce's hand and let go. The man turned to his bunk, dropped down on the thin mattress and tipped his hat over his eyes. Typical of the shy cowboy. The man had a painful stutter that worsened under stress. He'd rather fake sleep than carry on a conversation.

Pierce stepped past the first two bunks and nodded at the kid. "You're new here."

The blond-haired, blue-eyed gangly boy shook Pierce's hand with a surprisingly strong grip. "Name's Toby Gentry. You might know my oldest brother, Jake. I think you two went to high school together in Medora."

A smile spread across Pierce's face. "He played football, didn't he?"

Toby grinned. "Starting quarterback for three years straight."

"You'll have to tell him hello for me next time you see him."

"I will. We Skype once a week. Jake's in the army now, deployed to Afghanistan." Instead of a sad look, Toby's shoulders straightened, his thin chest pushing out, pride for his brother apparent.

The fourth ranch hand sat on his bunk, an unlit cigarette dangling from his lips. He didn't get up to greet Pierce. Instead his eyes narrowed.

Pierce refused to back down. "Hi, I'm Pierce Thunder Horse."

The younger man's nostrils flared, but he gave a nod of acknowledgment. "Ethan."

"I'll be helping Ms. Carmichael through the roundup."

"Whatever."

Toby motioned Pierce toward the bunk beside his. "You can bunk here."

"Thanks." Pierce unfolded the thin mattress and dropped his bedroll on it, eying the sullen ranch hand as he settled his sleeping bag. "I'd better get back up to the ranch house. The boss said she'd have a sandwich for me."

"I'll go with you. I'm kinda hungry, too." Toby led the way.

Pierce followed the boy out of the bunkhouse.

When the door shut behind them, Toby glanced at Pierce. "Don't worry about Ethan. He's not the friendly type. Likes to work alone."

Pierce fell in step with the young man. "What's his problem?"

Toby shrugged. "He's always been kinda a loner, but he ain't been right since his girlfriend died a couple months back."

"What happened to her?"

"From the little he's told us, she was in a fire or somethin'." Toby scuffed his boot in the dirt. "He doesn't like to talk about it and we don't ask. No sense in poking a man where he's hurting already."

Pierce could definitely understand that, and in spite of himself, he felt a little pity for the morose young man. "Thanks for the warning. Does he always have such a bad attitude?"

Toby's brows wrinkled. "Well, he ain't all that friendly, but he wasn't hired to chat. He does his job and he don't talk back. Don't know if he's planning on sticking around, though. Miss Carmichael hired the two of us on as temporary until she gets some fences mended and all the cattle in. If the sale goes well, we might stay on for good. If not…" his shoulders raised and lowered "…guess I'll be looking for work again."

"Does Ethan have a last name?"

"Mitchell. He answered Miss Carmichael's advertisement. Came from Bismarck. I think he has some local friends, though. Saw him talkin' to Shorty Duncan on his day off."

Pierce slowed. "Deputy Shorty Duncan?"

Toby turned to face him. "Somethin' wrong with that?"

"No, no. Just seemed odd. When was this?"

"Last Sunday." Toby's head tipped to the side. "Why?"

"No reason. Just curious."

Toby stepped up on the porch and strode toward the back door. He knocked.

"Come in," Roxanne called from inside.

The door opened into the large kitchen.

Roxanne stood at a butcher-block cutting board, wearing the same dusty jeans she'd worn all day, her feet bare and her auburn hair hanging down around her shoulders in wild, loose curls.

She'd taken time to scrub clean her face and arms and she looked young, sexy and so beautiful it hurt Pierce to look at her.

When she glanced up, her frown swept upward in a smile for Toby.

Pierce's fists clenched, the stab of jealousy completely unexpected and unwarranted. He had no claim to Roxanne anymore.

"Hey, Toby," she said. "I'm glad you came up to the house. I have some extra chicken here—could you use a sandwich?"

Toby grinned. "Thanks, Miss Carmichael. I sure could. Abe cooked tonight and it wasn't nearly as good as what you make. Not that I'm complainin'. Just saying."

She handed one of the two sandwiches she had prepared to him and the other to Pierce.

"Won't you have a seat?" She motioned for Toby to sit at the long solid pine kitchen table.

"Nah, but thanks. I think I'll eat this on the way back to the bunkhouse. It's gettin' late, and I wanna catch some shut-eye. Got a long day ahead."

Roxanne smiled and held the door for the young man. "See ya in the morning, then." She stood staring out at the night for a few minutes before she turned back into the kitchen.

Pierce laid the sandwich on the cutting board and sliced it down the center, handing her one side. "Eat."

"I'm not hungry."

"Do it for the ranch then. Your hands won't

want to play nursemaid to you if you pass out from malnutrition."

She glared at him, but she took the sandwich and bit into the end of it.

"What do you know about Ethan Mitchell?"

"Only that he works hard, and came from Bismarck." She bit off another piece and chewed. After she swallowed, she asked, "Why?"

"He's got a chip on his shoulder. I just wondered if you knew why?"

"Started a couple months ago. Apparently his girlfriend was killed in an accident back in Bismarck. Happened around the same time as Mason…" Roxanne set the sandwich on the cutting board. "Why do you want to know?"

"Have you ever said or done anything to make him angry?"

"No." She shook her head. "He's been a little bad tempered, but it never really seemed aimed at me. I assumed he was going through a grieving process."

"Angry for two months? You'd think he'd have moved on by now."

Roxanne's mouth quirked up on the corners then straightened. "It's not that easy, and you know it."

Pierce stared down at the sandwich in his hand. "Guess you're right. I'm still angry over my father's death, and at the sheriff for not doing any more than he did to investigate." Pierce's fingers tightened around the sandwich, as images of his father's body being laid out in the Thunder Horse ranch house crowded into his memory. The mix of anger, frustration and crushing sadness had meant that he'd wanted to lash out at everyone in the immediate vicinity.

Yeah, he could understand Ethan's anger. Pierce glanced at Roxanne. She'd been angry when they'd told her about Mason's death. Pierce had been angry as well—at himself—and he'd lost none of that anger or self-blame since.

He'd understood when Roxanne called off their wedding. But his heart had still broken, and not just from her rejection. Mason had been his friend, too. He'd grieved for the loss, as well, and mourned even more that he couldn't hold Roxanne through her sorrow.

Roxanne wrapped her arms around her middle and turned to stare out the window at the night. "Maybe you'd better go get some rest like Toby. We'll be up early tomorrow."

Pierce took his sandwich and left the kitchen, feeling no closer to bridging the chasm that had opened between him and Roxanne the day her brother died. Nor was he sure he wanted to bridge the gap.

She deserved better. Someone to be there for her, not someone who'd let her down.

As he headed back toward the bunkhouse, he tossed the sandwich into the bushes. After the eventful day, hunger for food was the farthest thing from his mind. Hunger for Roxanne? Well, he'd just have to get over it.

Chapter Seven

Roxanne headed toward her bedroom determined to follow her own advice and get to bed early. When she passed by her office, she remembered the stack of correspondence she'd put off as long as she could. Had all gone well today, she'd have tackled it as soon as dinner was over.

Tired to death and heart weary, she wanted to pass the door and ignore the bills, but she couldn't. If she didn't pay a couple of them, she'd be turned over to a collection agency. Not only would they hound her for payments, her credit rating would suffer and she'd never get another loan to tide her over through the rough months when cash flow was an issue.

Dragging her feet into the office, she sat behind the desk and stared at the mound of envelopes and the ancient computer on which she kept the ranch's books.

She opened the first envelope. A bill with a thirty-days-past-due notice. Her gut clenched.

Her father had prided himself on always paying his bills on time.

"Well, Daddy, a lot has changed and I'm not so sure you left the ranch to the right person."

Her father hadn't had much choice. Roxanne had been one of two children. Mason had had an equal interest in the ranch, but he hadn't wanted to stay and work it, preferring to join the FBI instead. That left Roxanne to take care of the ranch, the cattle and horses, not to mention her responsibilities as the Bureau of Land Management representative in charge of monitoring the wild horses of the badlands.

Roxanne loved the ranch and couldn't imagine herself doing anything other than what she was doing, but sometimes the struggle to keep things going was almost more than she could bear. Especially when the bill collectors came to call and she couldn't afford to pay.

The economy had tanked, cattle prices fallen and her mortgage had come due. The sale of the cattle would only stall the inevitable. Sooner or later, she'd lose the ranch and be homeless and jobless.

Then why the hell didn't she just get up from her desk and go to bed and sleep until next Wednesday?

Because Roxanne Carmichael didn't give up. It wasn't in her blood. She came from a long line of hardheaded Carmichaels who didn't know when to call it a day.

Determined to find the money to pay the bills, she tapped the keyboard.

Nothing happened.

She checked the plugs and the connections and tried rebooting.

The computer wouldn't reboot, the screen remaining dark.

Self-pity slammed into her like a mini-tsunami, crashing over her and sucking her down.

Tears filled her eyes. She rose from the chair, a rush of anger bubbling up and over. Roxanne shoved the stack of papers off the desktop and slammed her palm on the scarred wooden surface. "What next? Good Lord, haven't we suffered enough?"

With the walls closing in around her, Roxanne flung open the French doors leading out onto the deck and stepped through. She breathed deeply, hoping to calm the rising panic.

"How will we survive? How will I pay the men?" Roxanne dropped into the porch swing, burying her face in her hands. "I should just give up."

PIERCE DIDN'T MAKE IT back to the bunkhouse. Instead he performed a perimeter check of the ranch house and the outbuildings, circling each structure, checking inside, around the outside and anywhere danger might lurk.

He found nothing.

Before returning to the bunkhouse, he made one more pass around the ranch house. A light burned in the kitchen and one in the study. Roxanne was probably still awake.

Pierce wondered why. Was she worried about Jim? Suffering from insomnia after being shot at and almost getting caught in a landslide?

A soft sobbing sound reached him. He tilted his head to listen. Had it been the rustle of the leaves in the tree shading the house from the moonlight?

The breeze died down and the sobbing continued, accompanied by the repetitive creak of metal on metal from the direction of the porch.

Easing his way up the steps, Pierce tiptoed across the wooden planks until he stood in front of the old porch swing he and Roxanne had shared on many occasions.

The woman sat hunched over, her face buried in her hands, moonlight glinting off the moisture spilling through her fingers.

Seeing Roxanne, an incredibly strong woman, reduced to tears of despair tugged at Pierce's heart. All his self-made promises to keep a distance faded away as he reached out and pulled her into his arms.

Roxanne gasped, her eyes widening.

When she realized it was him, she stiffened. "What are you doing here?"

"I heard you crying."

She sniffed. "Cowgirls don't cry."

"Right." Pierce thumbed away a trail of tears on her cheek. "Must have been the wind I heard in the trees."

She sniffed again, her eyes pooling with a fresh wash of tears. "What am I doing wrong?" Roxanne buried her face against his shirt, her fingers clutching at the fabric. Her shoulders shook with each sob, the sounds muffled against his chest.

He stroked her hair and held her steady, comforting her, whispering words of his ancestors into her ear, soothing her.

When her tears slowed to a trickle, he tipped her face up and pressed a gentle kiss to her forehead. "Everything will be okay."

"How do you know?" She stared into his eyes, her own red rimmed and glazed with moisture.

"Because you're strong. You always come through."

Her head dipped, her gaze dropping to where her hands rested on his chest. "I'm not strong enough to protect my ranch and the people who work for me."

"You shouldn't have to worry about that. Let the sheriff find the shooter. It's his job."

She gave him a confused look, and for a moment, he wondered if she had other problems, troubles that she hadn't shared with him. But her expression closed off before he could analyze it further. "You of all people are one to talk. You never trusted the sheriff's investigation on your father's death. Why should I rely on him now?"

She had a point.

"These men can take care of themselves. You aren't their bodyguard."

She shoved her hair out of her face. "But they work for me. I'm responsible."

"Then give them the choice. Tell them what's going on, and then say that they can work for you and run the risk, or walk." Pierce cupped her chin. "You can't take care of everyone."

"But—"

"You can't," he said softly.

The fight seemed to go out of her, and she leaned into him. "I want to," she murmured. "I know it's wrong. But I can't help it. It's who I am."

"The person I fell in love with." Pierce laced his fingers through her hair and pulled her closer. She melted into him and he slid his finger under her chin, tilting her face up toward him before leaning in closer...closer...

A rustle in the bushes made him freeze, his head jerking up. He listened, trying to make out the noise.

Then a loud crash broke through the night.

"What the hell?" Pierce jumped to his feet and bolted off the porch, racing around the side of the house. He thought he saw a shadowy form running away, but before he could get a lock on where the person was going, there was a burst of light that dazzled his eyes and completely disoriented him. Turning his head toward the source, he let out a gasp of shock.

Someone had set the house on fire. And they'd started with Roxanne's bedroom.

RECOGNIZING THE SOUND as broken glass, Roxanne had rushed into the house as soon as Pierce had left the porch. Running into her room, she was shocked and horrified to see smoke and flames rising up the side of her bed, licking at the fabric of the quilt her mother had made especially for her.

"No!" Roxanne rushed forward, grabbing a throw rug from the floor, using it to beat at the flames, ignoring the way the acrid scent of gasoline filled her lungs along with the smoke.

"Roxanne!" Pierce called out through the shattered window. The next thing she knew, he'd barreled into the room, too.

Flames spread from liquid spilled on the wood flooring, and climbed up the curtains on either side of the broken window.

Roxanne yanked the quilt from the bed and tossed it to the floor, smothering the flames beneath her rug.

Pierce ripped an area rug up from the hallway and laid it over the flaming fluid, snuffing out the fire. Then he opened the broken window, yanked the burning curtains, rod and all, from the wall, and shoved them out onto the ground.

After the fire was out, Roxanne stood in the bedroom surveying the wreckage, her heartbeat finally slowing from the panic she'd felt only moments before. A fresh breeze helped clear the smoke from the room. Roxanne coughed, noticing for the first time the burning sensation in her lungs when she breathed. She stared at the damage. "Why is this happening?"

"I don't know," Pierce said. "But it has to stop."

Roxanne bent to lift her mother's quilt and inspected the damage. A giant scorch mark marred one corner, the rest was only blackened by smoke. A good washing would clean it up. But would it erase the stench of smoke? The lingering taint of fear?

She hugged the blanket to her body.

"I'm going to call the sheriff." Pierce headed down the hall.

"Miss Carmichael, you okay?" a voice called from outside the house.

"Yes, Toby," Roxanne answered. "I'm fine. I'm coming out."

While Pierce placed the call, Roxanne briefed the ranch hands on what had happened.

"Sorry, boys, but the sheriff will probably question everyone. I ask you all to cooperate."

Pierce stood on the porch, his gaze taking it all in.

Roxanne wondered what was going on behind his dark gaze. Did he have any lingering regrets that their moment together on the porch had been interrupted?

Outside, with the cool North Dakota night breeze chilling her skin, Roxanne had been having second thoughts. Perhaps the interruption had been destiny's way of saying *don't go there*.

The men returned to the bunkhouse and waited for the sheriff to arrive. Denying the urge to clean up the mess in her bedroom, Roxanne made a pot of coffee and sat on the porch, pretending to drink a cup, lost in her thoughts on where she and Pierce had been headed and the damage done both between them and to her house.

Twenty minutes later, Deputy Shorty Duncan showed up and took their statements. He gathered the bottle fragments, dropping them into an evidence bag.

"Someone used an accelerant and what looks like a beer bottle to make a Molotov cocktail."

He brushed his hands off on his trousers and met Roxanne's gaze. "Easy enough for even a grade-school kid, and damaging."

"Tell us something we didn't know," Pierce said.

"I'll have the bottle fragments dusted for prints." The deputy stepped back, his gaze panning the room. "No guarantees."

"I've heard that before. When are you going to actually do something about the man trying to kill Miss Carmichael?" Pierce asked. "After she's dead? No wait, you don't even investigate murders, do you?"

"You got a problem with me, Mr. Thunder Horse?" Shorty Duncan puffed out his barrel chest and moved toe-to-toe with Pierce. The deputy stood six inches shorter than the Lakotan, but he was no less self-assured.

Roxanne's pulse raced, sure she would witness a fight if she didn't do something. She eased between the two men. "Look, guys, I'm tired and I want to get some sleep in what's left of the night." She stared up at Pierce, holding his gaze.

"I'll do my job, just keep him on a leash, will ya?" Shorty snapped a few pictures, using a camera he'd brought from his SUV. "If you have any more troubles, just call nine-one-one."

Roxanne nodded. If they didn't find prints on the glass, the deputy's trip to her ranch would turn out to be nothing but a waste of time. At the rate the sheriff was investigating what had happened, someone was sure to die before they resolved the case.

It was time to take action.

After Deputy Duncan left, Pierce helped her clean up the glass and mop the remaining gasoline from the floor. When they'd finished, the clock had pushed past midnight.

With a full day of roundup ahead, Roxanne groaned. "I'm getting a shower. You don't have to stay. You can go back to the bunkhouse."

Pierce shook his head. "You take the first shower. I'll grab my gear and sleep on the couch."

Too tired to argue, Roxanne nodded. "Thanks."

"I'm just glad I was here."

"Me, too." She avoided his eyes and ducked into the laundry room where she gathered clean if wrinkled clothing that didn't smell of smoke. She hurried down the hallway to the guest bathroom.

She rushed through a shower, scrubbing the smoke and soot from her hair. Her chest felt tight, her throat raw, but thankfully the smoke in her room hadn't been too thick.

When she'd combed the tangles out of her hair and smoothed cream into her skin, she stepped out of the bathroom wearing a T-shirt and sweatpants. Nothing at all sexy.

Pierce had been to the bunkhouse and returned

with his bedroll. He'd removed his shirt and had just set his boots beside him on the floor.

When he straightened, Roxanne's breath caught in her throat at how big and handsome the man was. He wore his Lakota heritage with pride. She cleared her throat. "The shower's yours," came out in a gravelly croak. "Towels are in the cabinet beneath the sink. If you need anything else, let me know."

Roxanne stood for a moment longer, unable to tear her gaze from him.

He inhaled, his nakcd chcst expanding, then he let it out on a sigh. "It's been a long day. Go to bed, Roxanne."

As if all the wind had been sucked from her lungs, Roxanne hesitated only a moment longer. Then she performed an about-face and escaped into the guest bedroom, shutting the door firmly between them. She leaned against the wood panels, her heart racing, her body on fire with flames hotter than any Molotov cocktail could inspire.

Hell yeah, it had been a long night, and likely it would get even longer.

Chapter Eight

Pierce lay awake into the night, kicked back in the recliner in the Carmichael Ranch living room. His thoughts hadn't strayed far since he'd returned to the badlands. All centering on Roxanne, her bright auburn hair and incredibly blue eyes.

Two months had done nothing to shake her from his thoughts and dreams. Being with her again only reawakened the longing, making it stronger than before. If he'd thought he could just walk away from her, he'd been wrong.

He must have slipped into a troubled sleep, because the sun rising up over the horizon spilled into the living room of the ranch house, nudging him awake.

Shouts outside had him up and moving across the floor to peer through the window at the rear of the house.

The ranch hands had their horses gathered in the barnyard and were climbing into their saddles. Toby glanced toward the house, said something to Abe and nudged his horse, sending it forward.

Pierce shoved his feet into his boots and his arms into his shirtsleeves, buttoning as he strode through the house to the back door.

Toby arrived on horseback at the back porch as Pierce stepped out.

"Would ya let the boss know we'll be rounding up the cattle in the north pasture?" The horse danced sideways and Toby pulled the reins tight before continuing. "No need for Miss Carmichael to get out this mornin'. We can handle it."

Pierce nodded at the boy. "Good, because she'll be staying around the ranch house today, helping me with repairs."

"I will?" a voice said.

Pierce didn't have to turn to know Roxanne stood behind him. "She will."

Toby glanced from Pierce to Roxanne, his cheeks reddening. "Either way, we'll be back around sunset." He turned and rode away at a swift trot.

Pasting a smile on his lips, Pierce turned to face Roxanne.

Her curls lay around her shoulders, tousled as if she'd just risen from bed. She still wore the T-shirt and sweats from the night before. Twin flags of color rode high on her cheeks, and her blue eyes practically snapped at him. "Look, cowboy, this is my ranch and I'll call the shots."

He saluted and strode past her into the house. "Then call them. I have work to do in order to make your house temporarily livable."

She grabbed his arm as he moved past. "And I have cattle to round up. No cattle means no lights or payday."

"Like the cowboy said, they have it covered." Pierce held back a grin as he played his trump card. "Do you want Jim to come home to all this smoke damage? Might give him a coronary on top of his other injuries."

Roxanne let go of his arm, her eyes narrowing. "No, of course I don't want that."

"Right, then I'll need a hand getting it all cleaned up and ready. I'll bet the hospital will cut him loose this afternoon. He's bound to hear about what happened—can't expect the ranch hands to keep it to themselves—but if we clean up the worst of it, then we might be able to calm him down. But we'll need to have the place ready or he'll try to ride out after the bad guy himself."

Her gaze shifted to the window, her fingers twisting a long strand of hair. "I hate it when you're right." The stiffness leached out of Roxanne's body. "Since you're so smart, you can cook breakfast."

"I can handle that." He went one way, Roxanne the other.

In the kitchen, Pierce found the skillet and rummaged through the refrigerator for eggs and ham.

By the time Roxanne emerged in a clean pair of jeans and a faded and wrinkled chambray shirt that was two sizes too big for her, Pierce had omelets on the table.

"I loaded the washer with my smoky clothes. Remind me to switch the loads before I head out to the roundup. Mmm, that smells good." She pulled up a chair and lifted a fork, digging in.

Pierce loved that about Roxanne. She wasn't a girlie girl who picked at her food. She rode hard, worked harder and ate to keep up her strength. Add to that the pale face of an angel and auburn curls a man could lose himself in and...

Pierce swallowed hard and reined in his thoughts and desires. He wouldn't get much done at this rate.

They passed the meal in silence.

As soon as the dishes were cleared, Pierce headed for the barn, collecting hammers, nails, plywood and a circular saw.

When he returned, Roxanne was busy scrubbing the soot off the walls with a vinegar-and-water solution. She'd stripped the bed and tossed the sheets and the damaged quilt into the laundry room.

"You don't waste time," he commented.

Without pausing, she quipped, "Got cattle to get to the market."

"The men will handle it."

"It takes more hands than their four pairs and I've only got two more days to get the job done."

"Or what?"

"I miss the sale."

She started to say more but clamped her lips shut and went back to work on the walls. Making her way around the room, she cleaned the walls and then started in on the ceiling.

Pierce knocked the remaining shards of glass out of the window frame, careful to collect all the pieces and put them in a box to be recycled later. He cut a square of plywood out of the scrap he'd found in the barn and fitted it into the window, nailing it to the window frame, finding it strangely sad when the board blocked his view of Roxanne. Up until that moment, they'd been working quietly together, neither speaking, but for Pierce's part, he didn't feel it was an uncomfortable silence. He liked being around her. The woman wasn't afraid of work, whether it was washing walls or roping steers.

After returning the tools and remaining supplies to the barn, he entered the house through the back door.

Roxanne's voice drifted through the hallway from the ranch office. Her tone was one of distress.

His need to protect this woman pushed Pierce forward. He stopped before the door, out of sight but within listening range. Guilt over eavesdropping gnawed at his gut, but the need to help won out.

ROXANNE HAD BEEN ELBOW deep scrubbing the walls and the ceiling when the phone in the office had pulled her away from her task.

She'd answered the call, thinking it would be the hospital with news of Jim.

"Ms. Carmichael?"

"Speaking."

"This is Mr. Palmer from the First Bank of Medora."

"Hello, Mr. Palmer." Her stomach twisted into a knot and she sat in the chair behind the desk, bracing herself for what came next. "Did you get my application for the line of credit loan?"

"We did, and we've reviewed it." He paused. "I understand you've had some problems out there at the ranch."

"Nothing major," she lied.

"We received word that your foreman is laid

up in the hospital with multiple injuries and is unable to perform his duties." The man paused waiting for her to confirm or deny.

"And?" Roxanne asked, her voice terse.

"We also heard there was a fire and some damage to the ranch house last night."

Roxanne wasn't surprised. News traveled fast in small communities. She'd bet good ol' Deputy Duncan had passed on that little tidbit. If not, perhaps the dispatcher had shared the only incident on a boring night over coffee at the diner.

Her patience wearing thin, she cut to the chase. "I'm sorry, Mr. Palmer, I have a busy day ahead. Is there a point you're trying to get to?"

"Ms. Carmichael, in light of the recent events, the bank executives and underwriters have reviewed your request for the line of credit and have determined you to be high risk."

Blood drained from Roxanne's head and a ball of lead settled in her belly. "High risk? What does that mean?"

"That you are too much of a risk to loan the money to."

"I've always made my mortgage payments on time. I've never declared bankruptcy. I'm good for it. I just need a temporary loan until I can get the cattle sold."

"We understand, but in your case…"

Roxanne rose from the desk chair, blood boiling, her fingers clenching the handset so firmly her knuckles turned white. "In my case I'm a woman running a ranch in a typically male environment. Well, Mr. Palmer, let me tell you—"

Keep your cool, her inner common sense implored.

Roxanne caught herself before she spewed all her frustrations out on the telephone. She clamped her tongue between her teeth so hard she could taste the coppery flavor of blood.

Clearing her scratchy throat, she started over. "I'll be in town soon to discuss the situation with the bank president. Have a nice day," she ended, forcing the words between clenched teeth.

"That won't be necessary—" Mr. Palmer started.

"Oh, yes it will. Thank you, Mr. Palmer." She hit the end button and threw the phone across the room. It hit a shelf full of books then crashed to the floor and broke in half, the plastic pieces falling to the floor with a loud clatter.

Roxanne turned toward the French doors, staring out into the bright sunshine, and wondered how the sun could keep shining so optimistically when her world was falling apart.

"Anything wrong?" Pierce's voice cut through her thoughts, reminding her that she had more than a couple of unresolved issues in her life, her ranch finances and the attacker being two, Pierce Thunder Horse making it three.

With her back to the infuriating man she planted her hands on her hips. Her heart thumped hard inside her chest, feeling like it might explode. "Have you stooped to eavesdropping now?"

"Couldn't help overhearing. Is the bank giving you troubles?"

"No. Everything is perfectly *fine*." She pushed through the French doors and out onto the porch, needing to get away from him, from the banker and from everyone who pulled at her.

The thickheaded man didn't get the hint. He followed. "If you need a loan, I'm sure the Thunder Horse Ranch can front you the money to tide you over to the sale."

She spun to face him, closing the distance to stand directly in front of him. "Get this straight, Mr. Thunder Horse, I. Don't. Need. Your. Money. Or *anything* else from you." She poked his chest with her index finger on every word. "Not now, or ever."

He captured her wrist and held it, his black eyes so intense she felt them burn a hole right through her. "Are you that proud you'd risk losing everything you've worked so hard for just to save face?"

"I don't want to rely on you or any man. I can do this on my own."

"Damn it, Roxy, you're making it hard for me to help you."

"I didn't ask for your help," she said through gritted teeth. "I didn't want you to come back into my life."

"Well, that's too damn bad. I'm here and there's not much you can do to make me go away until this mess is resolved."

She stared up into his eyes, all the heat of her anger making her breathe hard, her chest rising and falling, pressing against his arm with each time she inhaled. As angry and frustrated as she was with him, it was still hard to fight her body's natural instinct to lean in closer to him.

His dark gaze bored into hers, sucking her into that black abyss. He seemed to be struggling, too. "I didn't want to come back into your life, but you make it hard for me to resist."

They were so wrapped up in the electric connection between them that the sound of a horse's hooves didn't register until the beast whinnied and snorted.

Roxanne glanced up, her eyes glazed, barely able to focus on the man astride one of her horses.

Ethan sat in the saddle, his hands gripping the reins, his eyes narrowed and, if Roxanne wasn't mistaken, angry.

She pulled away from Pierce and ran a hand through her hair. "What is it, Ethan?"

He hesitated, his hands clenching and un-clenching around the leather straps in his hands. "I came back for some more fencing supplies to repair the corral."

Roxanne frowned. "You know where they are."

"Right." He nudged his horse with his heels and the animal leaped forward, heading for the barn.

If not for Ethan's interruption, she might have thrown herself at Pierce. What was wrong with her?

"Roxanne—" Pierce's hands rested on her arms and he tried to turn her to face him.

She shook free of his grip and stepped out of reach. "I need to get out on the range and help with the roundup. We're done here."

THE NOTE OF FINALITY IN her voice made Pierce let go.

Roxanne reentered the house, picked up her cowboy hat and hurried toward the barn.

Torn between leaving and following her, Pierce made the only decision he could. He followed, jogging toward the barn, worried that she'd get so far ahead of him that he wouldn't be able to catch up or find her. She was still in danger, the target of an idiot bent on some evil revenge or something equally insane. He hadn't figured it out yet, but he needed to soon.

At first he'd thought maybe it was something to do with the horses or the canyon. But with the attack moving to the ranch house, it looked more and more like Roxanne was the target, not the wild horses of the Dakota badlands or anyone within the vicinity to the canyon. Narrowing down the targets should make it easier to find the attacker, but in spite of that, Pierce couldn't claim to be pleased with the latest piece of the puzzle.

At least out on the open range, he'd see a threat coming at them from a long distance away.

Pierce swung by his pickup and grabbed the rifle and scabbard he'd loaded in the rack behind the backseat. If there was trouble ahead, he wanted to be ready.

Roxanne led her mare from the barn, the saddle hanging loose on the mare's back. She tied the animal to a hitching post and cinched the girth.

"What horse do you want me to ride?" Pierce asked.

"None," Roxanne answered through gritted teeth.

He shrugged and entered the barn, gathered a lead rope and came back out to the pen where the horses gathered, hoping for a snack or a bale of hay to munch on.

He selected a large black gelding, snapped the

lead on his halter and opened the gate to bring him out.

By the time he'd captured his horse, Roxanne had the bit between her mare's teeth and was buckling the bridle behind the horse's ears.

Knowing he wouldn't get his gelding saddled in time to catch her, Pierce stopped in front of her. "Wait for me."

"I'm just going out to the north pasture. The others are out there now, moving the cattle. I'll be safe. You don't have to come."

"You're a stubborn woman."

"And you're an equally stubborn man." She swung up into her saddle and dug her heels into the mare's sides, sending her speeding off across the prairie.

"Damned woman." Pierce led the horse into the barn and threw a saddle on him.

He hoped he could find Roxanne quickly. On a spread the size of the Carmichael Ranch, that could take some doing. At least he knew what general direction she'd chosen.

Out in the barnyard, Ethan Mitchell was loading supplies onto a four-wheel-drive all-terrain vehicle, tying them down with bungee cords.

"I thought you'd be helping the others rounding up cattle," Pierce said.

Ethan ignored Pierce, climbing onto the ATV.

Pierce stood in front of the vehicle, determined

to get to the bottom of Ethan's bad attitude toward him. "Did I do something to piss you off?"

Ethan glared at him and revved the engine. "No time to sit around jawing—I've got work to do." The ATV leaped forward, missing Pierce by inches.

Anger burst through Pierce's veins, but he had more important matters to attend to. Pierce mounted his horse and rode out in the same direction as Roxanne, hoping she hadn't altered course.

She had ridden off without anyone watching her back. If Pierce didn't find her soon, there was no telling what might happen.

Chapter Nine

Roxanne headed out across the prairie, just as she had a thousand times before. Alone, without a bodyguard. But for the first time ever, she felt nervous and downright paranoid. Every noise, every shadow made her jump. Not until she caught up to the rest of her crew did she settle down.

She found three of her ranch hands working the herd, guiding them toward the pens closer to the ranch house. Once they had the entire herd in the pastures closer to the road, the animals would be corralled and loaded up to be transported to market.

The herd wasn't as large as it had been earlier that summer.

She rode up to Abe, settling her horse into an easy walk beside his. "Where are the rest of them?"

"All we can guess is that they made their way

down into the canyon. Won't be easy getting them out."

"Damn." She needed all of the cattle brought in so that she could cull those that would go to market and those that would stay back for breeding stock for next year's herd.

"We'll have to move what we have into the holding pens today. Tomorrow we can work the canyon. It'll take every one of us."

Abe nodded. "Won't be easy. Too many places they can hide."

"W-w-what a-a-about th-th-the message in th-th-the b-b-barn?" Fred asked.

Roxanne pinched the bridge of her nose, willing her headache to go away. "We have to try. We won't stick around long—just get the cattle and leave. And no one's to go out there alone, is that understood?"

She hated the thought of putting her ranch hands in harm's way, but the sale was too important to let any of the herd go unaccounted for. Especially with the bank denying her loan application. The money in the bank might reassure the powers to be that she could run a ranch, despite the troubles of late.

Troubles that were impossible to forget as long as Pierce Thunder Horse kept hanging around, she thought as she watched the Lakotan ride up.

As least he seemed willing to work. Without Jim, they needed every set of hands they could get.

PIERCE FELL IN STEP WITH the others, locating strays and bringing them into the herd, moving the cattle to the pen.

Chasing after one particularly stubborn steer, Roxanne got separated from the others. After leading Roxanne on quite a chase, the animal was finally trotting off in the right direction to rejoin the herd when Roxanne realized just how far she was from the ranch hands and Pierce. If any danger popped up, she couldn't just shout for help. They'd never hear.

She wondered how long it would take for Pierce to notice she was missing and come looking for her. Hopefully she'd get back before then. She was just turning her horse to return to the pen when a sound that didn't belong to the badlands reached her ears.

A motor's whine reached to her across the prairie.

Her mare danced in a circle.

A plume of dust rose from the dry earth as a dirt bike raced straight for her.

The biker maintained a direct path to collide with Roxanne and her horse, his speed insane, his body hunched low.

Cut off from her men, Roxanne raced the opposite direction of the dirt bike, hoping to make a wide circle and head back toward the ranch hands and safety.

She hadn't loaded her rifle and scabbard onto her horse, thinking she'd be fine working among the men all day. Hell, she wasn't used to bringing her rifle every time she went out to work the cattle. It wasn't supposed to be this way.

The faster her horse ran, the faster the motorcycle came at her.

The mare wouldn't last long at full speed. Roxanne had to do something before the cyclist came within range to shoot at her.

She topped a knoll and rode straight down into a copse of stubby trees. Swinging out of her saddle, she slapped her horse's hindquarters, sending her off in another direction, while Roxanne dove into the underbrush.

Seconds later, the bike burst over the hilltop, going airborne for a moment, then slamming to the earth, roaring ahead after the disappearing horse.

Roxanne remained hidden until the sound of the motorcycle vanished into the distance. She hoped her horse would find its way back to where the others were, or back to the barn. Whichever, as long as the animal was safe from the man on the cycle.

After five minutes of silence passed, Roxanne

rose from her hiding place and began the long trek back to where she'd left the men and the herd.

Halfway there, she spotted a lone horse and rider, galloping toward her. For a moment she considered ducking behind a tree or bush, but as she studied the way he sat straight and tall in the saddle, she knew it was Pierce.

When he reined his horse to a halt in front of her, his face was set in an angry scowl.

"You don't have to say it. I know." She stared up at him. "I shouldn't have left without telling you."

Without a word, he dropped down from his saddle and gathered her in his arms. She knew she should pull away, but after the near miss she'd had, she couldn't resist the allure of being close to him, feeling safe again even if it only lasted for a little while.

"You scared the crap out of me, you know that?" he whispered against her ear.

"I scare myself sometimes."

He leaned her away from him. "What happened?"

She tipped her head in the direction the attacker had gone. "The guy on the dirt bike came back."

Pierce held her at arm's length. "He didn't shoot at you?"

"Not this time. I didn't let him get close enough."

"Where's your horse?"

She chewed on her lip. "The barn, I hope. I ditched her and hid behind a bush. The guy on the bike chased her."

Pierce's lips curled into a smile. "I should be really angry with you." He tugged her close again, hugging her.

"You have every right. I should have paid more attention to how far I'd gotten from the group." She stared out across the rise, frowning. "I hope Sheba will be okay."

"Come on, your men will be worried." He mounted his horse and held out a hand for her.

She took it and, placing her toe on top of his, swung up behind the saddle.

They caught up with the hands as they neared the holding pen. No one questioned why she was riding double with Pierce and she didn't offer an explanation.

She slipped off the back of the horse, dropped to the ground and ran for the gate, throwing it open. The herd streamed through and raced across the pen to the other side where a gaping hole led out onto the gravel road beyond.

"Damn it! Abe, Fred, get over there and head them off before they get too far," Roxanne yelled above the sound of the cattle mooing.

Abe and Fred rode through the herd to the hole

in the fence and dropped down out of their saddles, ducked beneath the top barbed wire and out onto the road.

Roxanne looked around. "Where the hell's Ethan? I thought he was working the repairs on the fence."

"Haven't seen him since he went back for supplies." Toby eased in behind the herd and worked his way across the pen to the hole in the fence, blocking other cattle from making their escape.

Pierce herded the stragglers into the pen and closed the gate. "Missing someone?"

"Ethan." Roxanne shook her head. "Something's gotta give."

About that time an engine's roar sounded behind them.

Pierce and Roxanne turned as Ethan zoomed across the prairie toward them.

When he pulled up beside Roxanne and Pierce, Roxanne bit down hard on her tongue to keep from yelling at the man. "Where have you been?"

"Had trouble with the ATV. It quit working out in the middle of nowhere and took me a while to fix it."

"Seemed to be working fine when you raced out of the barnyard," Pierce said, his eyes narrow.

"And it's working now," Roxanne added, crossed her arms over her chest.

"Well, it quit for a long time. Had to jimmy a

few wires and fiddle with it to make it this far. You want these supplies or not?"

His antagonism triggered Roxanne's own anger. "You could have been here faster walking. Now, get over there and help the men gather the cattle who made it through the hole you were supposed to mend." She pointed to the broken fence.

Ethan swung his leg off the ATV and sauntered across to where the men were having a tough time getting the cattle back through the hole in the fence.

"I've a mind to fire him," Roxanne muttered.

Pierce nodded but didn't say a word.

While the men worked hard to retrieve all the cattle and mend the fence, Roxanne had Pierce take her back to the ranch house ahead of the others to prepare the evening meal. The men would be tired and hungry.

No words passed between them.

Roxanne cast a glance his way, noting the dark shadows beneath his eyes. He hadn't gotten any more sleep than she had. Tonight had to be better. She couldn't keep up this pace, especially with the grueling work of bringing in the strays from the canyon on the next day's agenda.

When they arrived at the barn, her mare stood waiting patiently for someone to remove the saddle from her back.

"I'll take care of the horses," Pierce said. "I know you have other work to attend."

She chewed on her bottom lip and sighed, too tired to argue. "Okay. But I don't like being beholden to you."

"You're not. Consider it a favor to the horses." His lips twisted into one of the crooked smiles that had always made her laugh.

Damn the man.

Roxanne hurried toward the house. Once inside, she slammed cabinet doors and pots and pans to relieve a little of the tension that spun up every time she was around Pierce.

She scrounged in the refrigerator, took stock of the contents of her freezer and almost cried. With barely enough staples to make a pot of stew for the men, her cupboards were frighteningly bare.

Doing the best she could, she threw the ingredients into a pot and had it ready by the time the men arrived, hungry and grumbling.

By the time they sat down to the table in the kitchen, it was dark outside. Roxanne had showered and was ready for a quick run into town, hoping to get there before the bank and the grocery store closed. A glance at the clock made her shoulders sag. Sadly, the bank would be closed. She wouldn't have a chance at talking to the bank president as she'd threatened Mr. Palmer. But she still needed to get to the store. Hopefully, she had enough room on her credit card to buy supplies for the pantry.

While the men consumed the stew, Roxanne gathered her keys and wallet. "I'm headed to Medora for supplies. I'll be back later."

"We're all out of sweet feed for the horses," Abe said. "And we're just about out of fuel for the ATVs, plus barbed wire and nails to shore up the pens and chute."

The more items Abe added to her list, the heavier the weight of her finances grew. She could only hope Mr. Batson at the feed and supply store would let her use her credit card or add those items to her account. She barely had cash to pay for the groceries she needed to feed her employees. She didn't even want to think about how she was going to pay their salaries.

Pierce blocked her at the door. "Wait until morning. The feed store will be closed."

"But I need to be out bringing in the stragglers from the canyon tomorrow."

"You're tired." He took the keys from her hands and turned her around. "Go to bed."

She wanted to, but there was so much riding on her. "I can't."

"Yes. You can."

He walked her back into the house and down the long hall to her bedroom. "Go to sleep. I'll clean up the kitchen."

For once, she didn't argue, too tired from all the hard work of the roundup, not to mention being chased by the bike and all the worry from her responsibilities closing in on her. Roxanne changed into a soft jersey T-shirt and crawled into her freshly laundered bed. The lingering stench of smoke was not enough to keep her from falling straight to sleep.

THE NEXT MORNING SHE WAS up early, ready to hit the road to town so that she could get back before most of the day was wasted. Pierce was nowhere to be seen. The couch didn't even look slept on.

Roxanne stepped out of the house and strode toward the barn to perform a flyby inventory of feed before heading to town.

As she emerged from the barn, Pierce joined her.

She stopped and faced him, guilt for taking up all of his time eating at her. "I don't need you to babysit me all the way to town."

"I don't consider myself a babysitter." He crossed his arms over his chest. "I like to think of myself as more of a bodyguard."

"Well, nothing's gonna happen today, and I'm only going to town. I seriously doubt anyone will try to harm me on my way in and back."

"I came out to tell you the hospital just rang. Jim is being released and needs a ride home."

Roxanne sighed, glad her foreman was well enough to come home but regretting the amount of time it would take to drive to Bismarck and back. "I'll have Abe get the supplies while I go pick up Jim." She started for the house, but Pierce's hand caught her arm.

"I have some things I want to check at the bureau in Bismarck. Let me get Jim."

Her brows narrowed. "You don't mind?"

"Jim's a good man. I don't mind in the least."

Roxanne stared harder at him. What was the catch? "You trust me to go all the way to Medora and back by myself?"

"Absolutely."

A truck pulled into the barnyard and stopped next to Pierce. Dante smiled and waved, then shifted into Park.

Pierce leaned close to Roxanne. "It's not you that I don't trust. It's the bastard who's trying to hurt you." He opened the driver's door for his brother. "My brother has graciously volunteered to take you to Medora for the supplies you need, haven't you, Dante?"

Dante's smile curved downward, his brows dipping. "I have? Mom sent me out to check on you two. She's been worried."

"And I have to make a run to Bismarck to pick up Jim from the hospital." Pierce clapped his brother on the back. "Perfect timing on Mom's part, wouldn't you say?"

"As I was saying..." Roxanne glared at Pierce. "I don't need a babysitter."

"She's got a point," Dante agreed. "She's all grown up."

"It's either go to Medora with Roxanne or stay here with her. Those are the choices." Pierce's mouth pressed into a thin line. "After the latest attack, I don't think she should be left alone."

"Yeah, heard about that." Dante's arms crossed over his chest and he gave his brother a tight look. "Mom heard from Sheriff Yost that Roxanne had another encounter with the dirt bike yesterday and that you had a little fire out here the night before. Nice to get that kind of news from the grapevine. Mom was not happy that you didn't call."

"The fire happened in the middle of the night. I didn't want to worry her."

"All it would have taken was a single phone call." Dante's arms dropped to his sides. "But I understand. Roxanne, are you ready to go?"

She stood with her feet braced, her arms crossed over her chest. "I don't need you to take me to town."

"The longer you argue, the longer it will take to get there and back. And I know you're dying to get back to the roundup." Dante hooked her elbow and tugged her toward the truck.

Roxanne glared over her shoulder at Pierce. The smirk on his face didn't make her any less mad. "Don't think you can order me around, Pierce Thunder Horse. I'm only going with Dante because it will take less time than me arguing with your sorry carcass."

"See you in a few hours. Don't go lookin' for trouble." Pierce tipped his hat and took off for his truck.

Roxanne climbed up into the cab of Dante's four-by-four pickup and sank into the leather seats. "I'm not happy about being babied." Not only did it put a hitch in her confidence, but it made her worry about how it would look to the bank president if he saw her being escorted by the Thunder Horse men, as if she couldn't take care of herself.

Still, she had to admit that it was nice not to have to be on alert for the whole drive. Even after a full night's sleep, she was still exhausted by the previous day's work and the thought of another tough day in the saddle ahead. She tipped her hat over her eyes and feigned sleep to avoid conversation with Pierce's brother.

Dante seemed as content to drive in silence as she was. By the time they drove into Medora twenty minutes later, Roxanne's muscles had relaxed and she'd almost fallen asleep.

Dante pulled into the feed store. A young clerk

was sweeping the front sidewalk as Roxanne jumped down from the truck.

"You can wait here," she told Dante. "I'll only be a minute."

Typical Thunder Horse, Dante climbed out of the truck and followed her in.

The teen frowned, set his broom aside and moved to let her by. "You're early, Ms. Carmichael."

"I have a couple things to get. It will only take me a minute."

With Dante in tow, Roxanne raced around the store, gathering nails and a roll of barbed wire.

"I need four sacks of sweet feed, too," she called out to the boy.

Dante helped the teen stack the four fifty-pound bags onto a hand truck. By the time they met back at the register, Roxanne had the items she needed.

The teen rang up the purchases. Roxanne handed over her credit card and held her breath.

Dante wandered off toward the hunting equipment and rifle cabinet, giving Roxanne a little much-needed privacy on her transaction.

After swiping her card twice, the clerk glanced up. "It's not going through."

Heat rushed up into Roxanne's face. She'd pushed her credit to the limit the last time she'd come to town. She'd hoped her credit card company would increase her limit just enough to allow the charges to go through. Glancing around at the items she had to have to keep her animals healthy enough to do the work they had to do, she sucked up her pride and asked, "Can I put it on my account?"

The clerk looked up her account number, entered the amount in the computer and shook his head. "Sorry, ma'am, your account is maxed out."

Out of options, Roxanne glanced down at the supplies. "I'm sorry to have held you up."

To Dante, she said, "I'll be getting groceries." Then she turned and left the feed store, her heart dragging around her feet.

She had to pass the diner on her way to the market. Mr. Palmer pushed through the door, almost hitting her in the face. When he saw it was her, he turned the other way.

"Mr. Palmer," she called out.

The man stopped and hesitated before he faced her. "Yes, Ms. Carmichael?"

"Do you know if the bank president will be in this morning? I'd like to set up a meeting about my line of credit application."

"As I said on the phone, it will be a waste of your time. The choice has been made. Nothing you can say or do will alter the decision."

"Without consulting me?" Her fists clenched and she stepped closer to the banker, standing eye-to-eye with the man. "What kind of bank are you running? Well, forget it. I'll find a bank that will loan me the money."

"Good luck with that, Ms. Carmichael. You're not a good risk—no one will loan you the money."

"You'll eat those words, Mr. Palmer. Just you wait and see."

Sheriff Yost emerged from the diner, his back to them as he spoke to someone inside. When he closed the door, his brows rose. "Is there a problem here?"

Anger still seething, Roxanne let Palmer escape as she turned her ire on the sheriff. "Yeah, what have you done to capture the man who shot at me and then tried to burn down my house with me in it?"

He raised his hands, a placating smile spreading across his face. "Now, now, Ms. Carmichael, we're doing the best we can. I have Deputy Duncan leading the investigation. I'm sure we'll get our man."

"Yeah. I'm reassured." She pushed past him. "In the meantime, I have to have a bodyguard because you can't do your job and keep the citizens of this county safe. Excuse me while I do something more productive than talk to a waste of taxpayer dollars."

Roxanne entered the supermarket, collected what little groceries she could afford, paid with the last bit of cash she had in her wallet and carried the bags outside to wait for Dante.

As she stepped out on the sidewalk, Dante's truck pulled up alongside her.

Good. At least she wouldn't have to stand around and risk running into more of the people who made her life hell. As she dumped the bags onto the backseat, she glanced into the back of the pickup at the four sacks of sweet feed and the roll of barbed wire she'd been forced to leave behind at the feed store.

Anger bubbled up yet again. She opened the passenger seat door and stared across at Dante. "Tell me you didn't pay for my feed and supplies."

"I didn't. I paid for your *animals'* feed and supplies." He grinned. "There is a difference."

She pointed toward the feed store. "Take them back."

"I can't."

"You sure as hell can."

"No, the store's closed until tomorrow morning."

"Liar."

His grin faded. "Roxanne, get in the truck, you're making a scene."

"I don't give a damn if I'm making a scene. I won't be the object of pity or charity."

"Then get into the truck." He shifted into Park and reached for his door handle. "Or I'll help you in myself. That'll make a nice, big scene if that's what you want."

"Damn you, Dante." Her voice shook as she climbed into the pickup and shut the door. "Damn you and all of the Thunder Horses."

"We've all been down at some point in our lives. I'm just trying to give you a hand up."

"I never wanted to be beholden to anyone."

"And you aren't now. Consider it a gift."

"It's charity."

"A *gift*." Dante shifted into Drive and headed out of Medora.

Roxanne sat in her corner, staring out the side window as the scenery raced by, fighting a wall of tears threatening to crumble around her.

Not far out of town, she leaned her face against the cool glass, wishing a hole in the ground would swallow her up. Her burdens had become so onerous she didn't think she could stay afloat long enough to swim to shore.

Perhaps it would be a blessing if someone finished her off. Then she wouldn't have to worry about the ranch being taken from her or where her next meal would come from.

Good grief, girl. Get a grip.

Roxanne sat up straight and swiped at the moisture in her eyes. Her daddy hadn't raised a quitter. Let her attacker bring it on. She'd be ready.

Chapter Ten

During the long drive to Bismarck, Pierce couldn't help but think about Roxanne and what had almost happened on the porch. If not for the fire...

He groaned. How was he supposed to stay focused on keeping her safe if he couldn't keep his hands off her? Maybe it was for the best for her to spend some time on Dante's watch instead of his. Without her distracting presence, Pierce might actually be able to make some progress on finding the man who was targeting her.

Pierce had called ahead to the hospital, letting them know that he'd be by to collect Jim after he stopped at the bureau. Tuck had been there working since he'd handed over the bullets, plastic and casings they'd found. While his absence—with a wedding to prepare for in less than a week—had to be driving his future bride nuts Pierce couldn't help but feel relieved that he could depend on his brother's help.

He pulled into the bureau parking lot in Bismarck and stared up at the building. It felt as if it had been months since he'd been there when, in fact, it had only been days. So much had happened at the ranch that he hadn't had time to stop and think. Some vacation.

Inside, he found Tuck at his desk, poring through computer files.

"Anything on the casings and bullets?" Pierce asked.

"Good to see you, too, Pierce." Tuck chuckled as he rose and hugged his brother. "They do match, but we couldn't lift any prints off them. Nor could we get a trace on the plastic explosives."

Pierce smacked his palm against the wall. "Damn."

Tuck resumed his seat in front of the computer. "I've been checking the databases on Roxanne's ranch hands. As expected, there's nothing on Abe and Fred. Clean as a whistle. But then you suspected that. They've been with Carmichael Ranch for a while. Toby had a speeding ticket a couple months back, but nothing alarming in his files."

"What about Ethan Mitchell?" Pierce leaned over his brother's shoulder and stared at the screen.

"Did you know he's a local boy from Bismarck?" Tuck clicked a few icons.

"Yeah, I gathered that much from Toby."

A mug shot of Ethan Mitchell appeared on the screen, his hair longer and dirtier, but with the same sullen face. "He had an arrest a while back for disturbing the peace. His neighbor called the cops when an argument took to the streets."

Pierce's chest tightened. "Convicted?"

"He paid a fine and that was the end of it. Apparently the woman he was arguing with was his girlfriend. He claimed it was a simple domestic dispute that got out of hand."

"What did the girlfriend say?"

"She refused to make a statement."

"Too afraid of him?"

Tuck shrugged. "Maybe. Probably. But I can't really say for sure."

"Nice to know the man respects women." His fingers tightened around the back of Tuck's chair, the urge to return immediately to the Carmichael Ranch so strong he had to fight himself not to give in.

"Yeah," Tuck was saying. "You should warn Roxanne that he might be trouble."

"Think he could have been the one who shot at her?" Pierce asked.

"I don't know. I didn't find any weapons charges against him."

"Dig deeper. He's got a real attitude. The man is surly, argumentative and rude."

Tuck snorted and smiled up at Pierce. "Making friends, brother?"

"See if you can find out where his girlfriend was."

"Why are you interested in her?"

"One of the hands thinks Ethan's got a chip on his shoulder because his girl died in an accident."

Tuck's brows rose. "An accident our friend Ethan caused?"

Pierce frowned. "Just dig."

"Will do." Tuck turned back to his computer. "Anything I can do from the ranch?"

Tuck shook his head. "Other than watching out for Roxanne, keeping an eye on Ethan and finding more evidence to go on…I can't think of a thing."

"I'm on it." Pierce straightened. "Let me know if you hear anything."

"Same with you. Some vacation you're on. You'll need to come back to work to rest up." Tuck rose from his seat and walked with Pierce to the door of his office. "Oh, one other thing. You need to stop by the tuxedo shop and check the fit on your tux for the wedding. Only a couple more days before *this* Thunder Horse ties the knot."

"I'll slip by on my way to pick up Jim at the hospital."

"Thanks, then I can tell Julia to mark you off her bad list."

Pierce chuckled. "Didn't know she had a bad list."

"She doesn't. Julia's an angel. I'm the bad guy, using my position as groom as an excuse to boss my brothers around." He smiled, his gaze on the photograph of Julia sitting on his desk. "She deserves to have it turn out great."

Pierce's chest tightened. "You love her, don't you?"

"Never thought I'd admit it, but I do. I think from the moment I met her over a year ago, I've loved her." He shrugged and grinned. "I was just too stubborn to see it."

Pierce had to force a smile. Seeing his brother so happy only made him realize how empty his life was. "Thunder Horse stubborn?"

Tuck clapped a hand to Pierce's back. "You got that right."

Pierce envied his brother's joy. "You're a lucky man."

"On that note, I'll agree. Now leave so I can get back to work. My fiancée would like to see me again before the wedding."

Pierce left the bureau building and drove straight to the tuxedo rental shop, whipping into the parking lot and shoving the shift into Park a little harder than was necessary. He was anxious to get back to the ranch as soon as possible.

Apparently Tuck had called ahead. The owner

pushed the door open as Pierce stepped down from the truck.

Within minutes he'd tried on the suit, confirmed that it fit perfectly, changed back into his regular clothes and been sent on his way, arriving at the hospital a few minutes later, coming to a stop in the drive-through pickup area.

Jim waited in a wheelchair inside the lobby, surrounded by the scent of disinfectant. There was a sheaf of discharge papers in his hands, and a frown creased his forehead. "About time you got here. Been stewin' in my juices for nearly half an hour. I could use a breath of fresh air. Damned hospitals. Can't stand the smell."

"Couldn't wait to go home?" Peirce asked, wheeling the chair through the door and out onto the curb.

"No, they couldn't wait to get rid of me," Jim grumbled, pushing to his feet. "And here I was about to make a move on the good-looking nurse."

"Probably why they booted you out of your room." Pierce wheeled the chair back inside and returned to help Jim.

In a hospital-provided boot, Jim limped toward the truck on his sprained ankle.

Pierce opened the passenger seat door and reached out to the older man.

Jim shoved his hands away. "I'm not a damned cripple. Let me do it myself."

Pierce stepped back as the man tried to maneuver himself up into the truck without applying pressure to the cast covering his broken arm, or the boot encased around his foot.

He grabbed the handle above the door and leveraged himself into the seat, dropping down with a wince.

Before the foreman could protest, Pierce leaned in, dragged the seat belt over his shoulder and snapped it in place across his lap.

Jim grunted his thanks, holding his injured arm out of the way throughout the process.

As Pierce headed out of the parking lot, the SUV's steering wheel pulled hard to the right. At first Pierce attributed it to the uneven pavement that took a beating during the winter's icy weather. But as Pierce maneuvered the truck onto the interstate heading west, the vehicle continued to pull to the right. He couldn't remember running into anything to knock the wheels out of alignment and the tires had all appeared inflated properly when he'd left the hospital.

He kept driving, determined to get to the ranch. He'd take the truck to his mechanic when he was sure Roxanne was safe.

"Miss Carmichael doin' all right?" Jim asked, taking Pierce's mind off the front wheel.

"She's holding her own. I sent Dante to Medora with her to keep her safe. She had some things to get and he promised to look out for her while I went to Bismarck."

Jim nodded. "I heard you had a fire in the house night before last."

Pierce shook his head in rueful resignation. He'd hoped they'd be able to keep the news from Jim, but really, he'd always suspected the man would find out. "How'd you hear about that?"

"I may be old, but I've got friends."

Jim had been a part of the western North Dakota community all his life. It didn't surprise Pierce that he had already heard about the fire, considering it was in the same house he lived in. "Someone tossed a Molotov cocktail into Roxanne's bedroom window."

Jim shot a concerned look his way. "Was she in there at the time?"

"No she was on the porch." *With me,* Pierce didn't add.

Jim's jaw tightened. "I don't know who the hell is trying to sabotage her life, but he'd better stop before I put a bullet right between his eyes."

"Believe me, if I knew who it was, it would have stopped already. He's not leaving much for us to go on." His fingers tightened around the steering wheel, his frustration bubbling up. Reminding himself that Jim didn't need more worry to add to his injuries, he asked, "What's the doc say about you and riding?"

"Not to ride horses." Jim breathed hard out his nostrils. "Didn't say nothing about driving a truck or a four-wheeler."

"You'll have a challenge driving with a sprained right ankle, and limited to one-handed steering."

"I'll manage. The cattle have to make it to the sale come hell or high water."

"Are things that tight?" Pierce asked.

"They ain't loose if you know what I mean. That girl's been working her fanny off to make that ranch pay enough to survive on."

A smile quirked the corners of Pierce's lips just as the truck jerked hard toward the shoulder, the right front end dipping toward the pavement. A loud screech ripped through the air as metal ground into concrete.

Pierce fought to keep the truck from careening off the interstate into a ditch. As fast as he'd been going, he couldn't maintain a straight trajectory. The vehicle slid off the road, bounced over the gravel and shot into the ditch, coming to a hard stop when the front end hit the embankment.

The force of the impact threw Pierce forward, the seat belt catching and stopping him from slamming into the steering wheel or flying through the front windshield.

When the world came to a complete stop, the

cab of the truck tipped forward at a steep angle, buried in the embankment.

Pierce shot a glance at Jim.

The man's seat belt held him from falling forward into the dash. His eyes were squeezed shut and his face was creased in a grimace.

"You okay, Jim?"

"Been better," he said through gritted teeth. "This seat belt is pressing against some of those broken ribs."

"Hang on, I'll get you out."

"I'm not goin' anywhere."

Pierce released his belt, falling hard into the steering wheel. He shoved his door open and scrambled out, ducking back to search the floorboard for his cell phone.

He found it lodged between his seat and the console. The screen was cracked and no manner of shaking or rebooting the device would make it work.

Tossing it aside, he hurried around the other side of the truck and pulled the door open.

Careful not to hurt Jim further, Pierce helped the injured man down onto the ground. Once he had the foreman settled, he rounded to the front of the truck and stared down at where the tire had been.

Both the wheel and tire were missing and, from what Pierce could tell, the axle had broken. A spare tire wasn't going to fix this truck; nor was he going to be back to the Carmichael Ranch anytime soon.

His chest tightened. Was it simply bad luck that the truck's wheel had fallen off? Or had someone loosened the lug nuts in an attempt to sabotage Pierce's truck and keep him from returning to check on Roxanne?

As soon as she'd stowed the groceries in the refrigerator and pantry, Roxanne headed for the barn.

Dante stood beside the truck, poking at the keys on his cell phone.

"You won't get any reception out here."

"A man can always wish." He glanced up. "Mind if I use your landline? I wanted to check in with Pierce and Tuck."

"Help yourself."

"I'll be just a minute. You won't go anywhere while I'm inside, will you?"

Roxanne shook her head. She'd ditched her bodyguard once too often lately, and what had it bought her? She'd nearly been run down by a motorcycle and buried in a landslide. "I'm not planning on going any farther than the barn for now. I'll stay put until you're done. But then I have to get out to the canyon. Today's the last chance I have to get those cattle into the sale."

As Dante jogged toward the house. Roxanne entered the barn.

While she'd unloaded the groceries, Dante had stacked the feed sacks inside the barn, but they still needed to be transferred into the right containers. Feed had to be stored in metal cans to keep the mice from getting into it. They could chew through a paper feed sack in less time than it took to pour the feed into one of the metal trash cans they kept for storage.

Hefting a fifty-pound bag onto her shoulder, she carried it across the barn to the row of cans lining the wall. Each contained a different kind of feed. She located the sweet feed can, tossed the lid onto the ground and tore open the sack.

As she emptied its contents into the can, the door to the barn swung closed, shutting out the daylight she'd relied on to see what she was doing. Assuming it had been the wind, she thought nothing of it beyond the inconvenience of pouring feed in the dark. Still, she knew the barn more than well enough to finish the task in the dark, so she didn't bother going over to reopen the door.

As she emptied the bag into the bin, the combination of oats, corn and barley along with the sweet scent of molasses filled Roxanne's senses. She'd always loved the smell of sweet feed. The horses loved it and needed the additional nutrition boost to keep up with the amount of work they performed during roundup.

As she laid the empty paper sack in the stack to be recycled, another aroma seeped into her consciousness.

The acrid, biting stench of smoke, coming from the back side of the barn where they kept the stack of hay bales they fed to the livestock on a daily basis.

Had something set off a fire in the hay?

A flash of concern sent her scurrying through the dark barn toward the door. She had to get outside and determine the source of the smoke and put it out before the barn went up in flame.

But when she pushed on the door it didn't open. She tried to lift the large wooden braces that locked the door in place—they wouldn't budge.

Smoke sifted through the walls. Sheba stamped her feet in her stall and whinnied.

"I know, girl." Roxanne spoke to the horse in a soothing voice, as much to calm her own nerves as the animal's. "I'm working on it. Something's jammed. It'll just be a minute."

No matter how hard she leaned on the latch, it wasn't going anywhere. Roxanne abandoned that exit and raced for the small side door. Again it wouldn't open, the lock jammed.

Smoke was filling the interior of the barn.

Sheba kicked the inside of her stall, her frightened cries echoing against the old oak timbers.

Roxanne ran her fingers along the wall beside the door and flipped the light switch. Nothing happened. Panic spiked as Roxanne realized this was no accident. Someone had started the fire on purpose—and beforehand, they'd deliberately locked her in. She raced back to the larger barn doors and pounded her hands against it. "Help! Someone help us!"

The men were out on the range, which left Dante as the only one who could free her from the barn. Surely he'd see the smoke rising and come out to help. But would he come soon enough?

Roxanne dragged in a deep breath to yell again. Instead smoke filled her lungs and she coughed uncontrollably. "Help!" she cried, coughing, falling to her knees to avoid the worst of it, praying for someone to come.

Roxanne crawled across the floor searching for something to pry the doors open. Then she remembered the pitchforks and shovels used to clean the stalls. Pulling her T-shirt up over her nose, she rose to a crouch and raced across the floor for the tools.

"We'll be okay, Sheba. Just hold on."

PIERCE AND JIM HITCHED a ride with a trucker on his way west. When they reached Medora, Pierce borrowed a car from a waitress he knew at the diner and drove the rest of the way out to the Carmichael Ranch, Jim beside him, his face pale but determined.

"I don't like it. Too many accidents to be considered accidental," Jim commented.

Pierce's thoughts exactly, and the reason he didn't wait to find a ride from Medora. Now as he turned onto the drive leading up to the Carmichael ranch house, his stomach clenched. A plume of smoke rose behind the house.

"You seein' what I'm seein'?" Jim sat forward.

"Damn." Pierce gunned the accelerator, shooting the little car forward. He skidded to a stop in the barnyard and leaped out.

Dante was running from the direction of the house, holding a hand to the back of his head, blood caked in his dark hair.

"What the hell happened?" Pierce asked.

"I don't know."

"Where's Roxanne?"

"Last she said, she was going to the barn."

Pierce ran for the barn door. A heavy metal lock held the latch in place. He grabbed it and yanked hard. "Roxanne!"

"Help. I'm in here." Her voice sounded thin, gravelly.

"Get a crowbar from my truck."

"You didn't drive your truck and I don't have a crowbar in mine," Dante said.

Pierce remembered his truck was somewhere between Medora and Bismarck, stuck in a ditch. With nothing around to break the lock, he had only one choice. He reached his hand out. "Give me your keys."

Dante dug into his pocket and handed Pierce the keys to his pickup.

"Get away from the doors!" Pierce shouted to Roxanne, then ran for the truck.

Chapter Eleven

Roxanne's first attempt to force the door by shoving the pitchfork between the two large doors and throwing all of her weight into it hadn't worked. The door hadn't budged an inch. She'd been on the verge of tears when she'd heard the voices murmuring outside, carrying through the thick wood doors of the barn.

Pierce's voice called her name. She forced herself to answer as loudly as she could, and was startled by his response. "Get away from the doors!"

She hesitated. Had she heard right? Her haze-muddled brain kicked in and Roxanne leaped to her feet. Smoke filled her lungs and stung her eyes as she threw herself to the side.

An engine raced, the sound moving toward her fast. Then the wooden doors exploded in a shower of broken boards and splinters as the hood of a pickup burst into the barn. Smoke spilled out through the opening.

The truck backed out through the hole.

Stumbling to her feet, Roxanne flung herself out of the barn and into a strong pair of arms. When she blinked the smoke from her eyes, she could have cried anew. Pierce held her, a fierce frown denting his beautiful brows. "Oh, thank God, you're here." She coughed and pointed back inside the smoldering interior. "Sheba. Please, help Sheba."

Pierce shoved Roxanne into Dante's arms and flung the damaged doors wide. Then he covered his nose and mouth with his arm and ran into the smoke.

He remained inside for what felt like a very long time.

Sheba's frightened whinny was followed by the smack of a stall door sliding sideways on its runners.

Sheba burst through the barn door, tossing her head and trotting as far from the flame-belching building as she could before she stopped and stamped her feet.

Roxanne held her breath until Pierce emerged, his eyes red rimmed and his face gray.

Jim hobbled toward her from a strange car parked in the barnyard. "Looks like it's comin' from behind the barn."

Pierce and Dante took off at a run, vaulting

over corral panels and ducking through fences to reach the back.

Roxanne followed, not as fast, her lungs burning from all the smoke she'd breathed.

When she reached the other side, Pierce and Dante were tossing burning hay bales away from the back of the barn.

Roxanne ran forward to help.

"Stay back—you'll get burned," Pierce shouted.

"So will you!" Roxanne continued forward.

"Just do it, Roxy. You've already breathed too much smoke." Pierce ripped the shirt off his back and beat at the flames licking up the wooden slats on the back of the barn.

Roxanne ran to the front where Jim was wrestling with a water hose one-handed. "Take this." He handed the hose through the corral panels.

She raced to the back of the barn with the hose while Jim turned on the water.

When she arrived, Pierce and Dante were in an all-out battle against the rising flames.

Roxanne aimed the nozzle at the fire and hosed down the wood, praying with all her heart that the thin spray of water would be enough. She couldn't lose the barn.

Pierce and Dante wet their shirts and beat at the burning hay bales, while Roxanne soaked the back of the barn. Slowly, the flames retreated, dying down to nothing more than wet charcoal by the time Roxanne was done.

With the hay bales scattered across the dirt, they burned down to ashes without lighting anything else on fire.

Roxanne stared at the charred barn, heartsick.

"It could be worse." Pierce slipped an arm around her waist and relieved her of the hose.

"Sheba could have died." Her voice didn't sound like her own, all gravelly and hoarse. She leaned into Pierce's side, pressing her face against his naked chest.

Pierce dropped the hose and held her close. "*You* could have died."

"But I didn't." She coughed, her lungs hurting, her throat scratchy and raw.

"You could have." Pierce led her around to the front of the barn.

Jim limped forward, his face pale and anxious. "You okay, Miss Roxy?" He hugged her carefully, his movements awkward with the cast.

Roxanne smiled at the older man. "I'm okay, just a little smoke-filled."

"Speaking of which." Pierce grabbed her elbow. "We need to get you to the hospital. You don't take chances with smoke inhalation. I should call for an ambulance."

"No. Don't. Really, I'm fine," she insisted, her

heart warming at Pierce's concern. "Just a little sore throat."

"You're at least going to the clinic in Medora. If the doc says you're okay, then you're okay. Until then, you're not."

She frowned. "I have cattle—"

"That can wait," Jim said, siding with Pierce. "Your health is more important than a few strays."

"You don't understand." Roxanne glanced from Jim to Pierce. Both had those stubborn looks, and she really didn't feel much like arguing. She could lose her ranch to the bank and they'd still stand firm on her seeing a doctor. "Fine. As long as Dante has to go, too. He looks worse than I do."

Dante had a hand pressed to the nape of his neck.

"Yeah, what happened to you?" Pierce turned his brother around and parted the hair at the back of his head.

Roxanne whistled, her stomach rolling. "You've got a lump the size of a goose egg."

"Yeah, and it hurts like hell." Dante rubbed the back of his head. "I was going to the ranch house to make a call when someone hit me from behind with what felt like a tire iron. I must have passed out."

All the blood rushed from Roxanne's head and she staggered. "Someone hit you?"

"Apparently whoever hit Dante probably wasn't trying to kill him. Otherwise, it would have been easy enough to take him out while he was unconscious. No, they just wanted him out of the way, so he wouldn't interfere." Pierce's frown deepened, his dark eyes icy. "This was a deliberate attempt on Roxanne's life."

The pounding of horses' hooves made Roxanne's head jerk up and she looked out across the pasture.

The four ranch hands raced toward them.

Toby arrived first, followed by Abe and Fred and finally Ethan.

"We saw smoke and came as quickly as we could." Toby dropped down out of his saddle and hurried up to Roxanne, stopping when he saw the destroyed barn door. "Holy smokes, are you all right?"

Roxanne smiled at the young man. "I'll be okay."

"What happened?" Abe dismounted, a frown creasing his forehead.

Roxanne sighed, not really feeling like going into it all. She just wanted to take a deep breath and have it feel good, instead of burning and making her chest ache.

Jim took over. "Someone started a fire in the stack of hay behind the barn."

Pierce gave a narrow-eyed look at the four

ranch hands. "When I get back from taking Roxanne to the clinic, I'll want a full accounting of where each of you were, down to the minute and GPS coordinate. Got it?"

Three of the four men nodded. Ethan glared, a sneer pulling his lip up.

Feeling she was letting her men down, Roxanne made the call to back off the roundup in the canyon. "I don't want you all out in the canyon until I get back and can ride with you. Someone's causing problems, and until we figure out who it is, I don't consider any of you safe." She turned to Jim. "Can you handle things here?"

"Yes, ma'am. Don't you worry about a thing." He patted her arm with his good hand.

Roxanne swallowed hard on the lump in her sore throat. "I'll be back as soon as possible." She stared at the ranch hands. "Work on getting this mess cleaned up and don't give Jim a hard time. He needs to put his foot up as much as possible."

With her final instructions issued, there wasn't much more she could do there. Roxanne turned to Pierce. "Let's get your brother to a doctor."

PIERCE HELD OPEN THE DOOR to the borrowed car for Roxanne. His brother climbed into the backseat, still holding a hand to the back of his head.

As he drove into town, Pierce's gut clenched. Who the hell was behind all the trouble on the

Carmichael Ranch? And just how many of the "accidents" were related? Had the same man sabotaged his car and attacked his brother just to keep them from protecting Roxanne?

"Whose car is this?" Roxanne sat up straight. "I hate to get it all smoky."

"It belongs to Rita from the diner in Medora."

Roxanne frowned. "Where's your truck?"

"Had a problem with the wheel on the way back from Bismarck."

"Sorry to hear that."

Dante leaned forward. "Did you get a chance to talk to Tuck in Bismarck?"

Pierce nodded. "No prints on the bullet casings or wrapper."

"That's too bad," Roxanne said, her eyes closed and her head tipped to one side.

Pierce reached out and touched her arm. "Are you okay?"

Roxanne opened her eyes and gave Pierce a lopsided smile. "Yes, I'm just resting my eyes. They're still burning from all the smoke."

Pierce's eyes still stung from the little time he'd spent going in to retrieve the horse. He could only imagine Roxanne's discomfort. "We'll have the doc check you over good."

Roxanne shrugged and closed her eyes again. "Did Tuck find anything else?"

Pierce glanced her way. "I had him run a background check on your employees."

Roxanne's eyes opened and she frowned. "And you didn't ask me?"

"It's routine in a case like this. You always look to the people closest to the victim."

"I would think I could tell you what you need to know about the men who work for me."

"Sometimes employers only know what the employees want them to."

"I'd trust every one of them."

"With your life?" Dante asked from the backseat.

Pierce could tell she wanted to say yes, but for once, Roxanne hesitated. "Usually."

"Did he find anything?" Dante prompted.

Again Pierce glanced at Roxanne as he said, "Ethan Mitchell has a prior arrest record."

Roxanne gasped. "He does? He didn't mention it when I hired him."

"The charges were minor. He paid a fine, and that was the end of it."

"Then why is there a problem?" she asked.

Pierce's gaze met hers for an instant. "It was for disturbing the peace during one hell of a fight with his girlfriend. Looks to me like he's got a problem with his temper."

Pierce didn't like breaking it to Roxanne. She'd

always been so trusting and open with the people who worked with and for her.

"He's never yelled at me." Roxanne's voice was nothing more than rough croak.

"Are you sure you haven't been the victim of his temper in other ways?" Pierce gave her a penetrating stare before returning his attention to the road. "An angry man can find a lot of ways to hurt someone, as you should be very familiar with by now."

Roxanne sat silently in her seat the remainder of the ride into Medora.

The clinic had already closed. Determined to get medical attention for both Roxanne and Dante, Pierce said, "We're going to Bismarck."

"No." Both Roxanne and Dante said in unison.

"Take us to where they house the ambulances," Dante suggested. "There should be EMTs there on call."

"Yeah," Roxanne agreed. "They should be able to help. It will give them something to do."

"They've had plenty here lately." Pierce frowned, not sure he liked the solution. He was outvoted, though, so he drove directly to where the ambulances were housed, calling on the expertise of the emergency medical technicians on duty.

After a thorough exam and observing Roxanne

and Dante for a full hour, the EMTs pronounced them fit enough to return home.

Pierce insisted on grabbing dinner at the diner since he had to return the borrowed car to the waitress who was due to get off work by then.

As they entered the diner Roxanne headed for the bar. "I'll call one of the hands to come get me and take me back to the ranch."

Pierce cut her off. "You and Dante sit. I'll take care of the call. Order me a steak and baked potato."

She frowned. "Bossy much?"

"Tired. And you have to be just as worn out with all that's happened in the past couple days." He motioned toward a booth. "Please. Let me handle it."

She sighed. "I don't want to get used to anyone organizing my life for me, but you're right. I'm tired." Roxanne gave him a little smile. "Medium rare, like usual?"

Pierce grinned. "That's my girl." He chucked her under her chin just like old times, when they'd been a couple and nothing could have separated them. Or so they thought.

The death of her brother had proved that theory wrong. He froze a little when he realized what he'd done, how he'd fallen back into old habits with her…but he pointedly didn't apologize before walking away.

While Dante and Roxanne slid into a booth, Pierce made arrangements he was sure would make Roxanne mad. He was through backing down when it came to her protection. If she wanted to yell at him for it, he'd deal with it. But he'd take the hit on a full stomach. Not before.

MUCH TO ROXANNE'S CHAGRIN and relief, Pierce paid the bill at the diner. By the time she'd finished a heaping helping of Ma Clements's famous chicken and dumplings, Roxanne didn't have the energy to argue. The smooth dumplings had slid right past her sore throat and hit bottom on her empty gut, filling her up and warming her inside and out. Sleepy and ready to call it a day, Roxanne left the diner, hoping whoever was coming for her from the ranch would be sliding up to the curb right about then.

A truck did pull up to the curb, but Maddox Thunder Horse was driving it.

Dante got in the front passenger seat and closed the door.

Roxanne stared down the street, hoping to see one of her men soon. She could barely hold her head up, much less stand for long. Sleep called to her and, despite the weight of the world resting on her shoulders, Roxanne was ready to give in. Tomorrow was another day. The cattle they'd rounded up already would have to do. Maybe the beef prices would be up on the day of the sale. She could always hope.

Pierce greeted his brother and opened the back door to the king-cab pickup. "Hop in, Roxanne."

"That's okay. I can wait here on the curb for my ride."

"This is your ride," Pierce said.

Roxanne frowned. "You have done more than enough for me. I can't keep relying on you and your family. Besides I'm sure my ride will be here momentarily."

"I called Jim and let him know that you won't be coming home tonight."

"You did what?" Anger beat out exhaustion as heat rose into Roxanne's cheeks. "I have to go back tonight."

"Jim said he had everything under control. They patched up the barn and made sure all the fires were out. He agreed you weren't safe there and that you should stay the night at the Thunder Horse Ranch."

Roxanne breathed in and out several times before she could speak in a normal tone. "You have no right to make that decision for me...."

"You've been shot at twice, almost run over and today someone tried to burn your barn down with you in it. You're safer at the Thunder Horse Ranch, Roxanne."

"But my ranch hands—"

"Right." Pierce pressed a finger to her lips to stem her next argument. "Jim made another really good point. With you off the ranch, your men are safer, as well."

"But what about everyone at the Thunder Horse Ranch? What about Julia? Lily? Katya? Your mother? Wouldn't I put them all in danger by staying there?"

"Julia's decided to stay at Tuck's place in Bismarck for now—with all the time he's spending at the office, it's the best way to see him, anyway. She and Lily will be safe there. Maddox won't let anything happen to Katya. And you know my mother too well to think that any amount of danger would keep her from helping a friend. It was her idea for you to come and stay with us."

Roxanne crossed her arms over her chest, hating that he made sense. "Seems you and Jim thought of everything."

"We tried," he said, grinning, "knowing you wouldn't like it."

She huffed. "Got that right."

"Can you two wrap it up?" Dante leaned out of the front passenger seat window. "I have a giant-size headache and it isn't getting better."

Pierce tipped his head to the side. "Now, are you going to keep Dante waiting?"

Outnumbered, outmaneuvered and overwhelmed,

Roxanne stepped up into the pickup and slid as far across the backseat as she could get. Sitting too close to Pierce would be a bad idea, even without her emotions on the edge and her heart hammering inside her chest. In her current state, Roxanne didn't trust herself, much less Pierce.

As they drove out to the Thunder Horse Ranch, the past few days' events crashed in around her. The danger to herself, and to others, reminded her how fragile life could be.

Despite the threats and attacks, the danger that scared her the most was the one to her heart, being near Pierce again. How was she supposed to remember that she couldn't rely on him if he kept being there for her every time she needed him?

Roxanne leaned her head against the cool window, closing her scratchy eyes. What a wreck she must be. She couldn't even summon enough anger to be mad at Pierce anymore. As far as she was concerned that was the most dangerous position she could be in. If she had a lick of sense and an ounce of energy, she'd make the Thunder Horse brothers take her home.

But Jim's insistence that her presence might put her men in danger hit too close to home—especially when she thought of how the danger had already gotten Jim hurt. Suddenly, she felt very alone, even in the truck with the Lakota brothers.

By the time the truck pulled into the driveway at the Thunder Horse Ranch house, Roxanne had sunk into a blue funk of colossal proportions.

All she wanted to do was shower and go straight to bed.

Pierce helped her climb down from the truck and insisted on taking her arm, leading her into the house.

Amelia met them at the door, clucking like a mother hen worried about her brood.

"Dante, sit," she ordered. "I want a look at the bump." She reached up and tried to part his hair.

"Mom, the EMTs said I'd be just fine." Dante waved his mother's hands away. "I want a shower before I touch anything. I reek of smoke."

Pierce chuckled. "She needs to mother someone, Dante. Let her."

"It's my job to worry. I'm your mother."

"Then worry about Roxanne," Dante insisted. "She's had the worst of it."

Roxanne shook her head. Though she loved Amelia Thunder Horse, she didn't want her to fuss around her. Pierce and his brothers would come and go, but Amelia was Roxanne's closest neighbor and the member of the Thunder Horse clan she interacted with the most. She didn't want the woman to see her as an object of pity. "I should go back home. I don't want to be a bother to you."

"Nonsense, dear. I'll find clothes you can wear." Amelia glanced at Pierce. "She can have my bedroom for the night."

"No, Mom, no need to give up your room," Pierce said. "She'll sleep in mine."

Roxanne's cheeks burned and she opened her mouth to protest.

Pierce cut her off before she could blast him. "Don't worry, I'll sleep on the couch."

"If you'll excuse me, I'll only be a few minutes in the shower." Dante hurried down the hallway.

"Oh, dear, you look like you've all had a rough day." Amelia led her down the hallway to the room that had always been Pierce's.

The room held too many memories for Roxanne. She'd hung out in his room on a number of occasions during their courtship. They'd lain together on his bed, kissing and touching each other, like teenagers. Out of respect for Pierce's mother, they saved the more intimate encounters for Roxanne's house where she was chaperone-free, but for her brother.

As Amelia pushed through the door, a flood of sadness threatened to overwhelm Roxanne. She stood in the center of the floor, unable to move, to speak or react lest she burst into tears.

Amelia flitted in and out, depositing a night-gown, clothes for the next day and a fresh towel on the end of the bed. The bed Pierce slept in, covered in a quilt his mother had hand stitched with pictures of wolves, buffalo, horses and other animals filling the big squares.

Everything about the room was masculine, from the rough-hewn cedar four-poster bed, down to the brown-and-black braided rug covering the hardwood floors.

"Dante is done in the shower if you'd like to go next." Amelia hugged Roxanne. "I'm so sorry you've had such a time of it. You're safe here. Let me know if you need anything else."

She backed out of the room, leaving Roxanne more alone than she'd felt since she'd called off her engagement to Pierce.

Things had been so good between them—and had then gone so terribly wrong. She'd told herself over and over again that she was fine on her own, that she didn't need anyone else, but now she was starting to wonder if that was true. Much as she hated to admit it, she'd needed Pierce over and over again during the past few days. And it wasn't just "need"—there was "want" to be considered, too. She'd never wanted any man like she'd wanted Pierce—like she wanted him, still.

But all of that was over between them...wasn't it? After the way he'd shut her out, and the way she'd vented her pain and anger on him, she didn't see how they could ever truly reconcile. And if they did, could she truly let herself trust him? Was there any way they could be fixed, or would she have to feel this alone for the rest of her life?

Chapter Twelve

The rest of the family settled in for the night. Maddox and Katya held hands all the way to their bedroom, and Dante suffered his mother's attention as she applied antibiotic ointment to his scalp wounds.

If all was well in the Thunder Horse house, then why the hell couldn't Pierce go to sleep?

Because Roxanne lay in his bed.

Images of her dark red curls feathering across his pillow kept him wide awake and aching.

When she'd skipped down the hallway after her shower, wearing the short filmy nightgown Katya had loaned her, Pierce thought he would come undone.

Now, as he paced the living room, he went over the events of the day, hoping the danger and turbulence would quell his desires and remind him what was important:

Keeping Roxanne safe.

He wanted to believe that nothing bad would

happen to her while she stayed at the Thunder Horse Ranch. That Pierce could go to sleep without worrying that someone was outside waiting to throw a firebomb through the window.

But could he? Who was to say that whoever had been responsible for the attacks on Roxanne hadn't followed her here to Pierce's home?

He suspected the wheel and tire problem he'd had on the road had been a setup to get him out of the way and keep him away from Roxanne for the day, just as knocking Dante on the back of the head had disposed of him.

His pulse thrumming faster than usual, Pierce slipped on his boots and stepped outside. One last pass around the house should help to ease his mind.

The cool night air felt good against his skin. He hadn't bothered with a shirt, normally preferring to sleep naked. In deference to the females in the house, he'd slipped on a pair of boxers to sleep in. They covered what was necessary to appease his family's sense of propriety.

As he walked around the house in boxers and boots, he could imagine the spectacle he made. A chuckle rose up his chest that caught in his throat when he passed his room.

The French door leading out of his bedroom stood open. A rush of fear for Roxanne spiked in his blood, sending his heart racing.

He spotted a dark silhouette outside, moving in the shadows, easing slowly along the porch toward his open door.

In three giant steps, he'd closed the distance to the house. Bracing his hands on the porch rail, he vaulted over the edge and grabbed the intruder from behind, trapping the stranger's arms against his sides.

A feminine squeak caught Pierce off guard. The person in his grasp fought and kicked. Beneath a bulky robe, Pierce could feel the curve of breasts and hips.

"Roxy?" he whispered, and spun her in his arms.

Her hair hung down in her face, her soft, silky curls slipping free of the robe's collar, brushing against his hands.

She stared up into his eyes, her breathing ragged, her body tense. "Pierce?"

"Yeah, baby, it's me." His grip relaxed.

"Why the hell did you grab me?" Roxanne pressed a hand to her throat and leaned her head into his chest. "You scared me half to death." A shaky laugh barely dispelled the fear in her voice.

After a steadying moment, she pushed away from him, backed up to the porch rail and sat against a thick wooden beam. Drawing her knees up to her chin, she wrapped her arms around her legs. The robe fell open, exposing the flimsy nightgown and a generous portion of her thighs.

Pierce cleared his throat to keep from groaning. "Can't sleep?"

"I'm so tired, I could tip over this rail." She shook her head. "But I couldn't fall to sleep."

"Too much to think about?"

She shrugged. "Too much of everything."

He stood beside her and leaned against the same beam, staring up at the stars, wanting more than anything to draw her into his arms but afraid she'd push him away again. "The stars sure are bright."

"Yes, they are." Her voice caught and she sniffled.

Pierce's heart skipped several beats and he turned to face her, capturing her arms in his hands. "Are you crying?"

"I've told you before, cowgirls don't cry." Her head dipped and she sniffed again.

"Liar." He tipped her chin up. Moonlight glistened off the moisture on her face. "Come here."

He drew her to her feet and into his arms, resting his cheek against her hair. "What's wrong?"

"It's your room," she whispered against his bare chest.

His room? He tipped her chin up. "What about my room? Aren't the sheets clean? Is it too warm?"

"No, no, everything's perfect…except…the last time I was in your room…we made love."

His hand slipped beneath the robe, which he recognized now as his, and he pulled her close. "And why does that bother you?" He held his breath, afraid of her response but needing to hear it nonetheless.

"I feel tense, alone…sad." Her hands slid up over his chest, circled around his neck and pulled his head lower, until his lips hovered over hers. "Damn you, Pierce Thunder Horse, I miss you," she said so softly he almost didn't catch her words.

But he did hear and his body stiffened. "You called off our wedding."

She nodded. "I was angry, grieving. And you wouldn't talk to me, wouldn't share with me what you were feeling. You wouldn't even tell me what had happened, other than to say it was your fault."

Pierce wanted to hold her in his arms and make love to her more than he wanted to breathe, but he couldn't. "That's because it *was* my fault your brother died. I shouldn't have taken him on that raid. I should have done better by him—and by you. You need to marry someone who can be there for you. Not someone whose life is at the mercy of the bureau."

"The bureau." She leaned her forehead against his chest, trapping their hands between them.

"How much do you have to give to your country?"

"I love my work."

"And I love mine, when I'm not being shot at, run over or trapped in a burning barn." A shiver shook her body.

Pierce knew how scared she'd been. Hell he'd been as scared for her.

She pulled her hands free and wrapped them around Pierce's waist. "For now, all I want is for you to hold me. No strings, no commitment, just hold me until I go to sleep."

When she put it like that, Pierce couldn't say no. His determination to let go of Roxanne and allow her to live her life free of him and the bureau was pushed to the back of his mind.

His arms slipped beneath the robe, and he lifted her up and carried her back inside to his bed. There he laid her against the pillows, her fiery red hair dark against the white pillowcases, moonlight casting a soft blue glow over her pale skin.

His groin tightened. The night would be hard on him, but he couldn't turn his back on her. He lay on the bed beside her and gathered her into his arms.

Roxanne laid her cheek on his chest, her hand resting low on his belly, one leg draped over his thigh.

Pressing a kiss to her forehead, he tightened his arm around her. "Go to sleep, Roxy."

Her face tipped up to him, her lips parted.

He bent to kiss her lightly. "Just sleep."

She deserves more became his mantra through the long, heartbreaking night of lying so close to Roxanne, knowing he couldn't hold her forever. Understanding that their time together was limited to the time it took to determine who was after her.

He held her, without moving, long into the wee hours of the morning. Near sunrise, he kissed her forehead and slipped out of the bed. After a quick shower, he stepped into the kitchen.

His mother was already up and cooking breakfast for the family.

"Morning, Mom." He dropped a kiss on her hair. "Tuck left a message on my phone about a lead on Roxanne's case, so I'll be headed to Bismarck today to follow up."

"What about Roxanne?" his mother asked.

"Keep her here. It's too dangerous for her to go out on her own."

His mother frowned. "I can't hold her hostage."

"Don't offer her a ride and don't let her take a horse."

"Honey, you know Roxanne better than any of us. You can't keep her from doing whatever she pleases."

"Should I be involved in this discussion?" a quiet voice said from just outside the door to the kitchen as Roxanne entered.

Pierce spun to face her.

She wore his robe, her curly hair was rumpled, and she blinked sleepily. "Are you going somewhere?"

"Bismarck," he said.

She bit on her bottom lip then stated, "I need to get back to my ranch."

Before she finished her sentence, Pierce was already shaking his head. "You're not going anywhere."

Her brows rose, her lips tightening.

Pierce's mother clucked her tongue. "Told you." She went back to the stove to stir the scrambled eggs in the pan.

Pierce decided on another tactic. "I have business in Bismarck at the bureau. Can you be ready to leave in five minutes?"

Her hand rose to smooth her hair back. "I'm not going. The cattle—"

"Will survive without you. And your men can get them ready for loading."

"I need to be the one to cull the breeders."

"Jim will be able to watch from the sidelines. If you're not going with me, you need to stay here where you're safe."

She opened her mouth to protest, but Pierce

pressed a finger to her lips. "Where you go, trouble follows. I worry about you. You worry about your employees. If you go back to the ranch, which of your employees will be the next in collateral damage? If you won't stay because I want you to be safe, stay here to keep the others from being harmed. Nothing's happened since you've been here so I think whoever's after you doesn't know where to find you. But even if he figures it out, I'd feel a lot better knowing you were here with Dante and Maddox."

Roxanne sucked in a deep breath, her gaze locked with his. Then her chin dipped and she nodded. "Okay, I'll stay, but hurry back. I need to be there. The Carmichael Ranch has too much at stake for me to run scared."

Pierce wanted to trust her, but she'd given up too easily. "Promise you'll stay safe?" He gripped her shoulders, forcing her to look back into his eyes.

"I promise to stay safe."

He frowned, not totally convinced, but he let it go. "I'll be back as soon as possible." He hated to leave. Something in his gut told him that Roxanne would only be safe if he was by her side. But this new lead of Tuck's could be the answer to finding the guy behind all of this. He had to leave Roxanne in order to protect her.

So why did it feel so wrong?

ROXANNE WATCHED THROUGH the living room window as Pierce pulled out of the yard and disappeared down the gravel driveway.

"Don't worry, he'll be back soon." Amelia patted her back. "Pierce can't stay away long knowing you're in danger. He loves you so much."

"I doubt that." Roxanne glanced down at the shorter woman. "How can you be so nice to me when I dumped your son? I don't think I could be as gracious."

Amelia smiled and patted Roxanne's cheek. "Grief has a way of making a person a little crazy. You know, first there's the denial, then there's the anger." Amelia shrugged and moved away to gather magazines from the coffee table. "I think you were so heartbroken by your brother's death that you lashed out at the only person you could at the time. Unfortunately, it was Pierce."

Roxanne's gaze shifted back to the window. Had she pushed Pierce away in her grief? Did she still love him? "He told me it was his fault that Mason died."

Amelia nodded. "I'm sure he believes that. But he'd probably say the fire at your house was his fault, too. Do you agree with him?" Amelia held the magazines to her chest, her eyes sad.

"No, of course not. Why would he think it was his fault?"

"Because he didn't stop it from happening. I imagine he blames himself for Mason's death in the same way—thinking it's his fault because he was responsible for Mason and yet he couldn't protect him."

Was that true? Roxanne knew that Pierce was never one to pass the buck—he always accepted blame when he thought he'd been in the wrong. But was he blaming himself for things that weren't his fault, things that had never been in his control? She'd been so angry when Mason died that she'd never thought to question whether Pierce really had been to blame. Was there a chance that his mother was right?

"He wouldn't talk to me about the explosion," Roxanne hedged. "I still don't know what happened."

"Neither do I, dear. I was never able to get him to open up, either. But I do think he needs to talk about it, if someone's stubborn enough to get through to him." Amelia excused herself to go see to things in the kitchen, leaving Roxanne alone in the living room. She lifted a pillow from the floor and arranged it on the couch, at a loss for what to do with herself. Wishing she was out on a horse, the wind in her hair.

On an end table next to her was a photograph of Lily. Roxanne picked it up, staring at the image of the small child who looked so much like a little

Lakota papoose, her face pale, her pitch-black, straight hair pulled into a tiny tuft held by a pink bow-shaped clip on top of her little head.

Roxanne settled in a rocker-recliner, touching her toe on the floor to set the chair in motion as she stared at the photograph.

Looking at the image of the baby who so closely resembled her father, Pierce's brother, Roxanne couldn't help thinking *what if.* What if she hadn't called off her wedding to Pierce? She could be pregnant now. What would their baby have looked like? Would she be dark like Lily or would she have red hair like her mother? Would he be strong, with high cheekbones and dark skin like Pierce? Would he like riding horses or playing football?

The list of possibilities seemed endless and… useless.

A tear slipped from the corner of Roxanne's eyes as she rocked back and forth, the chair's gentle sway only reminding her of everything she'd given up. She still loved Pierce, but she didn't know what kind of future they could have. He'd more or less told her he didn't want her back. What kind of crap had he said? She deserved someone better?

Pierce was a man of character, a man who stood by his family and friends. Did that really go with the idea she'd clung to—that somehow Pierce had let Mason down, leading to his death?

Roxanne closed her eyes to the image of her brother's battered body lying in the coffin at his funeral.

"Are you okay, honey?" Amelia Thunder Horse appeared before her.

"I'm fine." She set the photograph back in place.

Amelia settled on the couch and took up a crochet hook and a half-finished afghan, her fingers twisting around the yarn as she poked the needle in and out of loops. "It sure has cheered up the house, having the baby here," she commented. "I have to say, I worried about my special agent sons—especially Tuck—wondering if they'd ever settle down enough to give me grandbabies."

"Why Tuck, in particular? Pierce is certainly very dedicated to his job. He loves being an FBI agent."

"True, but he knows there's more to life than that. You know Pierce tried to talk Mason out of joining the FBI."

Roxanne's head jerked up and she stared across at Amelia. "No, I didn't know."

Amelia's lips twisted. "You can't tell young people anything. They have to make their own decisions, find their own way."

Brushing away a stray tear, Roxanne nodded,

unable to speak, her heart hurting, the pain of her loss still fresh.

"Mason came over practically every evening for a week after he got accepted into the academy. He could barely wait." The older woman's lips lifted in the hint of a smile. "I remember trying to talk Pierce and Tuck out of joining the FBI. Lot of good it did. I heard them telling Mason the same things I told them—mostly that they needed to stay and run the ranch."

"That's what I tried to tell Mason."

Amelia glanced across at Roxanne. "Don't get me wrong, my boys all love this place. It's their home. But Pierce, Dante and Tuck wanted to follow their own dreams—they wanted to make a difference for others. I couldn't hold them back, even if I had wanted to, and I did want to. They had to live their own lives."

"And the ranch didn't fit in with their plans... or Mason's."

She'd blamed Pierce for so many things—was it just because she hadn't been able to accept the truth? She fought so hard to defend her right to choose her own life on the ranch. Had she held Mason back by not giving him the right to make that choice for himself?

"You might not have known that Pierce was the one to find Mason after that warehouse explosion."

Roxanne shook her head, the tears falling faster.

"He held Mason until the medical folks arrived. But Mason died in his arms." Amelia Thunder Horse brushed a tear from her cheek. "He never said anything. Tuck told me."

Roxanne's heart broke all over again, but in a strange way she felt healed. The anger and blame that had taken over, ruining her relationship with Pierce, had finally begun to lift. She could forgive him for everything that had happened...and maybe she'd be able to help him forgive himself. Amelia had said he needed someone stubborn to help him see the truth—and no one was better at out-stubborning Pierce Thunder Horse than her.

As soon as he entered the FBI building in Bismarck, Pierce went straight to his office. Tuck popped in while Pierce was booting up his computer.

"Remember that lead I said I was looking into?"

"Yeah." Tuck had Pierce's full attention. "Who is it?"

"The neighbor who filed the report that got Ethan Mitchell arrested."

"Ever get the name of the woman Mitchell was arguing with?"

"No, but I got the name of the police officer

who arrested him. He might know more about what happened."

"Let's pay the man a visit."

"I'm a step ahead of you, brother." Tuck grinned. "Got an appointment to have coffee with the man in fifteen. Grab your keys and let's hit the road."

Pierce led the way out of the building and climbed into the truck, Tuck sliding into the passenger seat.

Ten minutes later they pulled into a diner that had seen better days but had an impressive number of cars gathered in the parking lot.

"Must have good food," Tuck observed.

"Have to—the place looks like a dump." Pierce climbed down and entered the establishment, his gaze panning the busy restaurant for a uniform.

"He said he was off duty," Tuck informed Pierce.

A man sitting alone at a table waved at them as a waitress plunked a plate full of pancakes in front of him.

Pierce strode across the room and pulled out a seat in front of the off-duty police officer. "Pierce Thunder Horse." He stuck out his hand and shook the policeman's.

The man didn't apologize for eating in front of them; he just lifted his fork and knife and dug into the stack. "What can I do for you two?"

Tuck unfolded a printout of Ethan Mitchell's mug shot. "Remember this guy?"

The man nodded, chewing on a gooey bite of pancake. He swallowed. "Arrested him a couple months ago for disturbing the peace. From the looks of it, if I'd been about ten minutes later, I could have gotten him on assault, too. I got there just in time to keep him from getting violent."

"Why wasn't the girl's name listed in the arrest report?"

"She refused to give a statement. And we couldn't file any charges against her—she wasn't the one making all the ruckus."

Pierce leaned forward. "Did you ask the neighbors who she was?"

"They said she was his girlfriend, but they didn't know her name. She was always coming and going."

Pierce hid his disappointment. The cop hadn't been able to tell them much more than what was already in the report. "Sorry to interrupt your breakfast."

"I didn't know her name at the time of the arrest, but I think I know who she is. Saw a picture of her that same week in the obituaries."

Tuck glanced across at Pierce then turned to the officer. "You say it was the same week?"

"Yeah. It's been a couple months so I don't remember her name anymore. But I bet if you look through the obits for that week, you'll find her."

Pierce wasn't sure that knowing the name of Ethan's dead girlfriend would help, but he didn't have anything else to go on. "Thanks for your time." He passed on shaking the man's hand, preferring to let him finish his breakfast.

Back in the truck, Pierce sighed. "I feel like we're chasing our tails."

"You said to dig deep on Mitchell. That's what we're doing. You know your gut is your best investigation tool. If your gut tells you to look into Ethan Mitchell, that's what we've gotta do." Tuck clapped a hand on Pierce's shoulder. "Let's go to the newspaper office and see if we can access the obituaries for that week. They might find things faster than we can."

Pierce headed for the local newspaper office. Once there they waited ten minutes for someone to free up to help them dig through the files for the week Ethan Mitchell was arrested.

It had been a busy week of deaths.

Going through the newspaper stories for that week, Tuck sat back. "I remember that week. We were here in Bismarck." He looked up at Pierce.

At the same time, Pierce ran across the article reporting an explosion at a local warehouse. The blood drained from Pierce's face. "That was the same week as the raid."

He didn't have to say which raid. His brother knew…he'd been there. "The one where Mason died," Tuck finished.

Pierce sat back in his chair, the air knocked out of his lungs just as if he'd been punched in the belly.

"It wasn't your fault Mason died," Tuck said. "It could have been you or me in that warehouse. He just happened to get there first."

"I know that. We lost a number of good agents that day." And Pierce had lost his fiancée, as well.

"Look, Pierce, if this is too much to go through, I can finish."

"No." Pierce leaned forward and pressed on. "I'm fine."

"You don't look so fine."

"It's been a bad week."

"I'm sorry about you and Roxy. I never thought she'd blame you for Mason's death."

"It was my fault. I should have stopped him." Pierce shook his head. "It's just as well. We could never have made it work between us."

"How so?"

"She has the ranch. I have the bureau. What kind of life is that for a couple?"

"If you love each other enough, you can make it work."

"How?" Pierce shot a straight look at his brother. "She'd be in the corner of Nowhere,

North Dakota. Who knows where I'd be if she needed me?"

"It's a chance you take on each other. And there would be family close by if she needed help."

"She deserves someone who will stick around and be satisfied with ranching."

"What if she doesn't want to keep up the ranch?"

"It's her home. She's the last Carmichael. I would never ask her to give it up to follow me. She has dreams of her own."

Tuck nodded. "You have a point. Besides, she dumped you. It's not like the issue will ever come up again. She doesn't strike me as a woman who will come crawling back on her hands and knees."

"I wouldn't want her to," Pierce said.

"Do you want Julia to talk to her? She wasn't keen on marrying a special agent, but she came around."

"No." Pierce shook his head. "Just leave it. It's over between Roxanne and me."

"Doesn't look too over to me," Tuck muttered.

Pierce ignored him, flipping through the computer screen to the next day's paper and scrolling down to the obituaries. That's when he found a picture of a woman in her mid-twenties. He glanced at the name, Leah Jennings. "Tuck, why does this name ring a bell?"

"I don't know, but it does." Tuck leaned over

and stared at the picture. "I don't recall her face, just the name." Pierce hit Print and pulled the photograph and write-up off the printer. "We got what we came for here. Let's go back to the office and see what we find on Ms. Jennings."

Chapter Thirteen

Roxanne paced the living room and kitchen of the Thunder Horse ranch house, becoming more agitated with each hour that passed. Several times she'd called the Carmichael Ranch trying to get through to Jim, and each time she'd hung up frustrated when she'd gotten no answer.

Her foreman had just survived a significant fall with multiple fractures. He shouldn't be up and running so soon. And yet, if he wasn't, the work might not be getting done.

Guilt burned like bile in Roxanne's already scratchy throat. Standing on the porch, staring out over the pastures, wishing she could see all the way to her place, she had just about had enough of the waiting.

Maddox had made a run to town for feed, taking Katya with him. Dante had stayed behind, claiming he had reports to catch up on for his work with the U.S. Customs and Border Protection. Yet instead of holing up in the office, he'd gone out to the barn.

Roxanne suspected he only stayed because of her.

She hated being watched over like a child. And she hated even more that Dante had already been the recipient of her attacker's violence.

Roxanne gripped the porch railing, her fingernails digging into the wood. Inactivity made her crazier than not knowing who was after her. She needed to talk to her men and find out where things stood with getting the cattle ready for sale. In the bright light of day, it seemed crazy to think that she wouldn't be safe with her men—or that they'd be in danger just from having her there, especially if they all stayed together. Surely they could protect each other.

She'd trust Abe, Fred and Jim with her life. Toby and Ethan were newcomers to the ranch, but they'd been there for the past three months before the incidents started so she was sure they couldn't have been involved.

Not being there to keep an eye on the people and place that meant so much to her was killing her.

Amelia joined Roxanne on the porch and laid a hand on her arm. "They'll call if something happens that shouldn't. Why don't you come have a cup of hot tea with me? Or I could make up some lemonade, if you'd like that better."

She stuck her hands in the back pockets of the jeans that Mrs. Thunder Horse had laundered. Her clothes no longer had the acrid scent of smoke, but Roxanne couldn't get the smell out of her senses—a constant reminder of everything that had happened and of how easily her home could be taken away from her if she wasn't vigilant in protecting it. "No thanks. I really need to get home."

"Honey, you're not safe there right now. And you promised Pierce you'd be safe."

Roxanne closed her eyes. She had promised him that. But surely she'd be safe as long as she took precautions and stuck close to the men. They needed her out there with them.

If she didn't get the cattle to the sale, she wouldn't be able to pay her ranch hands. They'd leave for paying work and she'd be left to run the ranch on her own. She couldn't manage all the work by herself to earn enough money to pay the mortgage. All strikes against her.

She stood to lose her home and the ranch that had been in her family almost as far back as when Theodore Roosevelt had lived in the badlands. The cattle sale was her only hope, and she couldn't help with the roundup, all because someone was playing her.

Roxanne smacked the porch railing with her palm. "Horsefeathers!"

"Excuse me?" Amelia stared at Roxanne, her brows wrinkled. "Did you say horsefeathers?"

"I did. I'll be damned if I let my ranch be taken back by the bank or anyone else."

"Is the bank giving you troubles, dear?"

Already regretting opening her mouth, Roxanne scuffed her boot on the wooden deck. "Not yet. But they will if I don't make my mortgage payment. I need to be out helping with the roundup."

Roxanne grabbed Amelia's hands. "Please. I just need a ride over to my place. Or I could borrow a horse and bring it back tomorrow. Please, Mrs. T." She stared into the woman's eyes.

Amelia squeezed her hands. "Honey, you know I can't keep you here. You are not a prisoner. I only ask that you reconsider. Maybe Dante could go with you, to keep an eye out for you."

"Dante already took a hit for me. I can't ask him to take me."

"Maddox will be back shortly, I'm sure of it." In her concern, the older woman gripped her hands hard enough to hurt. "Can you wait at least until then? Perhaps Pierce will be back from Bismarck by that time, and he can take you himself."

More guilt washed over Roxanne. She'd already put two of Amelia's sons in danger watching over her. She didn't want anything else to happen to the Thunder Horses. With a sigh, she hugged Amelia. "Okay, I'll wait until Maddox comes back, or Pierce—whoever gets here first. Then I really must go home."

"Thank you, dear." Amelia hugged her back, her arms strong, reassuring. "I'd be so worried if you left without someone to watch out over you."

"I'm just not used to standing around, doing nothing. It's making me crazy."

"You could help me with lunch," Amelia offered. "Or maybe you'd rather help Dante out in the barn. At least you'd have something to keep you busy while you wait."

A shiver trailed across Roxanne's skin as she thought about the day before, being trapped inside the burning barn. If she hoped to get over the trauma of the fire, she could start in the Thunder Horse barn, where burning was less likely. "I'll find Dante. Maybe I could be of some use to him. No offense, Mrs. T."

"None taken, dear. Go."

Roxanne hurried down to the barn, ready to do something physical, anything to pass the time until Maddox or Pierce returned and took her back to her ranch.

Dante was bent over the unshod hoof of a black stallion, scraping it clean with a hook.

"Need a hand?" she asked.

"Not really."

"Okay, let me put it this way…." Roxanne took a deep breath and released it slowly. "Is there anything I can help with, to keep me busy before I blow a gasket? Please?"

Dante chuckled. "Bored?"

"More frustrated than bored. But yes."

"Then you can bring the bay mare in from the pen and tie her up to the next stall. Her hooves are in bad shape. I'm pulling shoes and cleaning. The farrier will be by later."

"I can do that." She grabbed a lead rope from a nail and hurried outside.

The next thirty minutes was spent in silence as the two pulled old metal horseshoes off the stallion and mare and cleaned the accumulated gunk out of their hooves.

"Dante!" Amelia Thunder Horse's shout made Roxanne drop the mare's last hoof halfway through cleaning.

Dante had just settled the stallion in a stall and given him a bucket of feed and a couple sections of hay. He stepped out of the stall and hurried to meet his mother outside the barn, pulling her into his arms. "What's wrong, Mom?"

Amelia Thunder Horse's hand shook as she spoke. "I just got a call from the sheriff's department. Maddox and Katya have been involved in a wreck. They're being sent to the hospital in Bismarck."

Her heart thumping hard against her ribs, Roxanne emerged from the barn, wiping her hands on her jeans. "How bad was it?"

"They didn't say, just that they were being taken by ambulance to St. Alexius in Bismarck. We should go at once."

"Come on, I'll drive." Dante led his mother toward the house, then stopped and turned toward Roxanne, frowning. "You'll have to come with us."

"No." Roxanne remained standing beside the barn. "You'll need room in the truck to bring Maddox and Katya back, if they release them immediately. And I want to be here in case Jim needs to reach me for anything. You two go. I'll stay here."

"But that leaves you alone." Dante shook his head. "No, you'll have to come."

"If anything happens, I know how to shoot a gun and I can call the sheriff." When Dante opened his mouth to protest, Roxanne held up her hand. "Go. You need to check on your brother and his fiancée. I'll be fine."

Dante's frown deepened. "You wouldn't try to go home, would you?"

Roxanne waved them on. "I'll just finish up

on the mare's hoof and get her settled. You two should hit the road. It's a long drive to Bismarck."

Amelia's brows knit. "I don't like leaving you."

"I don't like knowing Maddox and Katya are hurt. Please, go." Roxanne turned back to the barn, ending her side of the argument. By the time she'd finished scraping the mare's hoof, she heard the crunch of gravel in the driveway as Dante and his mother left for Bismarck. Roxanne wondered if Maddox and Katya's accident was caused by the same person who'd been gunning for her. More guilt piled into her already churning gut.

As she led the mare into a stall and fed her grain and hay, she couldn't stop thinking about what had happened in the past few days and how it didn't make any sense.

The shooting that had started it all made the least sense of all. Who had it out for her and why? Other than the land she owned, she couldn't come up with a single reason someone would want to kill her.

Was it the land? No one had approached her about purchasing the Carmichael Ranch. With times as tough as they were, not many people were stupid enough to invest in a small-time cattle operation that barely paid the bills.

Not many people except for her. Because it was all she had left of the family she'd loved.

A lump rose in her throat and she swallowed hard to clear it. She'd done enough moaning and crying over the loss of her family. And she'd let recrimination and bitterness lead her to pushing away Pierce, and her best chance to start a new family.

Now that she looked back over the past couple months, she recognized her actions for what they were. Anger over the loss of her brother and fear of investing her love in yet another person who stood a good chance of dying and breaking her heart.

Not that she was the only one to blame—Pierce had pushed her away, too. But if they were both willing to let go of the past, was there still a chance that they could build a future together?

A shadow passed over the door to the barn, blocking the sunlight.

Roxanne glanced up to see the silhouette of a man astride a horse.

She froze, unable to see the rider's face and whether or not he carried a gun.

"Ms. Carmichael?"

Roxanne let go of the breath she'd been holding and stepped forward at the familiar voice. "Toby?"

"Yes, Ms. Carmichael, it's me." He leaned over his saddle horn.

"What's wrong?" She emerged from the shadows of the barn and blinked in the bright light of day. Ethan sat on a horse a few paces behind Toby, his cowboy hat pulled down, shading his eyes. "Is Jim hurt? Are the others okay?"

"They're fine. Ethan and I were sent over to get you because one of the wild horses is down. We thought you should know, being that you're the representative to the Bureau of Land Management and all."

Roxanne stiffened. "Which one?"

"I'm not sure. Ethan saw her. He thinks it's Sweet Jessie, the one injured the other day when that man shot her."

Roxanne glanced at Ethan. "Was she down... dead...or still alive?"

"Still alive," he answered, his words terse.

"Where?"

Ethan touched the brim of his hat, tipping it lower, the shadow all but hiding his face. "Not far from the watering hole near the canyon rim."

"Ethan and I can try to doctor her, or—" Toby paused "—put her out of her misery, but we thought you'd want to call it."

A weight as heavy as lead settled in Roxanne's chest. Sweet Jessie had been one of her favorites. When they'd spotted her a day ago, she'd been up and running, as if the gunshot wound hadn't fazed her a bit. It must have been worse than they'd thought for infection to set in that quickly and take her down.

"I'm coming." Roxanne glanced around. "Can one of you saddle a horse for me? I need to run in and call Pierce to tell him where I'm going."

Ethan leaned forward. "No time. If you want to help her, we need to go now."

Roxanne frowned at Ethan's sharp words. "By the time you have a horse saddled, I'll be ready." She stared across at the younger man, her early thoughts resurfacing. But she pushed them aside, the horse's welfare more important than her own safety. "Find a horse in the pen over there. Don't saddle one from the stalls, they need shoes. I'll be back before you're done."

Toby dropped down out of his saddle and hurried toward the pen Roxanne had indicated. Ethan dismounted and strode into the barn.

Taking off at a run, Roxanne raced to the house and up the porch steps. She found the kitchen phone and tried calling Pierce's cell phone, but the call went straight to voice mail. Frustrated, she hung up and tried Tuck's cell, hoping that he'd be with Pierce and could pass the phone over to him. When she got his voice mail, too, she went ahead and left a message. Then she grabbed a pad of paper and a pen and quickly scribbled a note to Amelia explaining what had happened, in case she got home first.

Then she ran back to the barn.

Ethan was slipping the bridle over a mare's head while Toby cinched the saddle's girth around her belly.

Instead of mounting immediately, Roxanne ran into the barn, found the large-animal medical supplies and filled a saddlebag with items she might need. Pierce's family was just as involved with the care and concern for the wild horses of the badlands as she was. They wouldn't mind her taking supplies, especially in as big a hurry as she was. She'd pay the Thunder Horse family back when she could.

When she emerged from the barn, she tossed the saddlebag over the horse's hind quarters and tied it to the saddle with the leather straps. All in all it had taken less than eight minutes to run to the house and gear up.

She mounted and reined the horse around, aiming in the direction of the canyon. "Let's go."

They took off at a gallop, Roxanne in the lead. The ride seemed to take forever, with Sweet Jessie's fate in the balance. When they finally neared the border to the Carmichael Ranch, Ethan pulled up next to Roxanne. "We might need help holding her down."

Roxanne slowed to a stop, her gaze panning the landscape.

"Ethan, go get Abe and Fred. Toby and I will find Jessie and assess the situation."

"I saw her. I know exactly where she is. Toby can get the others and bring them back."

"Fine. Toby, go." Her thoughts were half a mile ahead on Sweet Jessie, hoping it wasn't too late to save the mare.

"Where should we look for you?" Toby asked.

"Around the watering hole near the rim of the canyon," Ethan answered.

Toby galloped away, leaning low over his horse.

As Ethan and Roxanne neared the watering hole, Sweet Jessie was nowhere to be seen.

"I thought you said Sweet Jessie was here."

"She was. She might have gotten up and moved down into the canyon to hide. Maybe she's trying to find a place to die. We'd better hurry."

Roxanne's throat tightened. Not Sweet Jessie, the filly she and Pierce had nursed through a storm. It would be like breaking the last link to their shared past. She nudged her horse, sending her to the canyon rim.

As they neared the edge, Roxanne glanced down the trail they'd used when Jim had been injured. "I don't know how we're going to get down in there. This trail is a mess from the landslide."

Ethan reined his horse to the north. "I know another way down." He followed the rim for several hundred yards before he nodded toward a rocky outcropping. "There's a trail on the other side of those boulders." He started down.

Roxanne had never seen this trail before, hidden as it was in a maze of brush and boulders. She was surprised that it was wide enough for horses to climb in and out of the canyon easily.

As they descended, Roxanne glanced around, keeping a watch out for men with guns. "You know, Ethan, I think it might be better if we wait until Pierce can ride down with us. I'd hate for one of us to get hurt."

Ethan shot a frown over his shoulder. "Jessie was really bad off. If we wait, she might not make it."

Roxanne looked above her at the canyon rim, wishing she'd waited on Pierce. But if Jessie was as bad off as Ethan was making her out to be, every minute counted. "Okay. Go." But she'd keep an eye on Ethan all the way, still unsure of him. Without a gun to protect herself, she could be riding into a trap. But then Ethan didn't have a gun on him, either.

She rode silently down the trail, working through all the incidents in her mind. Each time she'd been attacked, her ranch hands had been out in the field rounding up cattle—as far as she knew. Rounding up cattle on a large spread meant splitting up to find those animals hiding in the bushes. The ranch hands could have been scattered and busy enough they wouldn't see if one of them had slipped away.

The time she'd almost been run over by the motorcycle, Ethan had claimed the four-wheeler had broken down. Had he swapped the four-wheeler for a dirt bike to terrorize her?

As the trail leveled out onto the canyon floor, Roxanne pulled her horse to a stop and she stared across at Ethan. "Ethan, have I ever done anything to make you mad?"

He turned to face her. "No."

"Have I treated you unfairly?"

With a shake of his head, he nudged his horse. "Nope. These tracks might lead to the horse. Come on."

Roxanne moved out a little slower, letting the distance between her and Ethan lengthen, her gut telling her that being alone in a canyon with Ethan wasn't one of her brightest decisions. Either he was telling the truth, and he wouldn't be much protection for her, unarmed as he was, or he was working against her and she could be in danger. She reined in her horse. "I'm heading back to the Thunder Horse Ranch to wait for Pierce. It doesn't feel right down here."

Ethan pointed ahead. "There! I think I see her." He dug his heels into his horse and raced ahead.

Adrenaline shot through Roxanne's veins. As

Ethan's horse took off, her own horse couldn't stand being left behind. She tossed her head, trying to loosen Roxanne's tight grip.

"Okay, fine. We'll check it out. But if she's not there, we're heading back." Roxanne gave the horse her head.

The animal leaped forward, galloping along the rocky ground.

Ethan and his mount disappeared over a rise.

Roxanne tempered her horse's headlong rush to catch up, afraid she'd slip on the loose rocks and hurt herself.

As she topped the knoll, she spotted Ethan's horse standing still, its sides heaving, the saddle empty. The animal stood at a narrow choke point in the canyon, the walls pocked with an array of caves, some mere overhangs, others gaping entrances. Roxanne had spent many summers exploring the canyons with their father and Mason, but she didn't remember this place.

She eased her horse forward. "Ethan?"

"In here! She's in here!" His voice echoed off a cave's walls.

The sound bounced around the cliffs towering over Roxanne's head. "Where are you?" she called out.

"Follow my voice."

Roxanne dismounted and walked toward one particular cave. She led her horse by the reins.

The horses occasionally entered the caves to avoid the bitter winter winds in North Dakota, but it was summer. Sweet Jessie wasn't making sense, unless, like Ethan had intimated, she was looking for a place to die. "Ethan, come out so I can see where you are."

As she waited for him to appear, she glanced at the ground, searching for hoofprints of an unshod wild horse. Instead, she found narrow tire tracks.

Her breath lodged in her throat. "Ethan! Get out here."

She backed away from the cave's entrance, her pulse hammering through her veins. "Ethan. Please. We need to leave, right now."

Ethan stepped out of one of the larger caves, his right arm by his side, aligning with his right leg. "We're not going anywhere."

The tone of his voice sent chills along Roxanne's spine. "We need to go, it's not safe here."

He lifted a rifle in his arms and aimed it at her chest. "Correction...it's not safe for *you*."

Chapter Fourteen

Pierce sat in front of his computer, poring through the criminal databases, trying to find a match on Leah Jennings. So far, nothing. Ready to call it a bust and head back to the ranch, he tried searching the internet for the name in Bismarck.

His fingers tapped against the surface of his desk as he waited. Finally a string of hits popped up on his screen. The first was a high school yearbook photo of Leah Jennings from the local Bismarck high school, dated several years back. In the photo, she was a fresh-faced young woman with long sandy-blond hair who smiled back at him from the screen.

He clicked on another photo of a woman in a mug shot, her hair dirty and streaked purple and pink, piercings on her eyebrow, nose and ears. What made a young person go from girl next door to that? Probably drugs.

Farther down the list was a string of news headlines from a couple months back. He clicked on one and a picture popped up on the screen with a caption that knocked the air from his lungs.

Explosion Claims Lives of Four Feds.

He recognized the picture from one that had been plastered over all the newspapers and newscasts. It showed the night they'd raided the warehouse in Bismarck that had been used to store stolen and illegal weapons. The FBI and ATF had conducted a joint operation to expose and disarm a radical militia rumored to be preparing for an attack on government buildings across North Dakota, Montana and Minnesota.

Pierce had been the one who'd received a tip from a concerned citizen that the militia group would be meeting at a certain time to distribute weapons to their counterparts, using a warehouse in the southern part of Bismarck.

Because the tip had come to Pierce, he, Tuck and Mason had been assigned to assist the ATF in capturing members of the militia and seizing the weapons. At first, everything had gone according to plan. The ATF had lead on the bust, and Mason had insisted on volunteering to go in with them. Pierce and Tuck had set up a communications outpost on the outside. It should all have gone down smoothly.

What they hadn't counted on was the explosives hardwired throughout the building, set to go off if the warehouse was raided. It had all been a setup. Pierce had led the team into a trap. He'd received the tip and he hadn't questioned the validity or the possibility that it wasn't what it seemed. It had been his fault that Mason and the three ATF agents had died in that explosion.

Pierce's fingers curled into a tight fist, his eyes burning. Mason had lived long enough to die in his arms, his final request for Pierce to look out for his sister.

The memories washed over him like a black, murky wave of swamp water, dragging him down into the well of despair he'd experienced, knowing it was his fault and that he had to be the one to break the news to Roxanne.

The kicker of the entire event was that not all the arms the militia had amassed had been stored in that location. An entire arsenal of deadly weapons had been relocated only hours before the raid. Pierce's team had moved in faster than the militia had expected, otherwise there would have been no weapons or militia members in the building at the time of the explosion. But the bulk of the inventory—and the militia membership—was still at large, and no one knew where…at least, no one who was willing to talk.

"Anything?" Tuck leaned in the door to Pierce's office. "I checked criminal databases and didn't have a match.

His brother's voice yanked Pierce out of the

past and back to the article in front of him. "I'm reviewing old newspaper articles."

Tuck entered the office and leaned over Pierce's shoulder. "Damn. Isn't that—"

Pierce nodded, his empty stomach roiling. "The warehouse explosion."

"Why are you revisiting it?"

"I did a search on Leah Jennings in Bismarck and this was one of the articles that came up."

"Holy smokes." Tuck poked a finger at the screen farther down the page. "Says Leah Jennings was one of the members of the militia who died in the explosion. What kind of coincidence is that?"

The air left Pierce's lungs in a whoosh. "Leah died in the explosion?"

"You think Ethan has anything to do with the militia?"

"I don't know." Pierce opened another tab on the browser and keyed in "North Dakota Militia" and "Ethan Mitchell" and waited for the search engine to do its thing.

A moment later, several articles and images popped up on the screen, all of which had something to do with the militia but held no mention of Ethan Mitchell in particular.

Pierce pulled up photographs taken of a demonstration at the capitol of North Dakota by the local militia six months ago. He blew up the photograph and studied the blurred images.

"There." He pointed to the screen. "Isn't that Leah? The one with the purple streaks?"

"Could be. Who is that next to her?"

A young man in dark cargo pants and a slouchy jacket could have been Ethan, but his face was turned too far away to be certain.

"Move the picture to the left." Tuck's brows pulled together. "See what I'm seeing?"

Pierce tried to adjust the focus on the image, but it didn't get much better. "Looks kinda like…"

"Shorty Duncan." Tuck let out a long low whistle.

"What the hell was he doing at the rally?"

Pierce stood so fast his chair rolled back and hit the file cabinets. "When did the sheriff bring him on?"

"I don't know, but Mom or Maddox would."

"I have to get back to the ranch." Pierce grabbed his keys from the desktop.

"But we might find more information while we're here."

"Something doesn't feel right. I need to get to Roxanne." Pierce skipped by the elevator and took the steps down to the ground level, Tuck on his heels.

They climbed into the truck and pulled out of

the parking lot, Pierce driving, Tuck pressing buttons on his cell phone.

Before he could hit Send to place a call to the ranch house, his phone buzzed, indicating a couple of voice mails had come in while Tuck's phone had been in a pocket of bad reception.

Pierce strained to hear the message while negotiating the traffic.

Tuck hung up the phone with a muttered curse and stared across at Pierce. "Bad news."

His pulse shot blood and adrenaline through his arteries. "Give it to me."

"The first call was from Mom, letting us know that she got a call from the sheriff's department saying Maddox and Katya had been involved in an accident and were on their way to St. Alexius hospital here in Bismarck."

Pierce's heart jumped into his throat. "A car accident? Was their car tampered with, too?"

"Mom didn't say. She didn't seem to think it sounded too serious, but she did say that she and Dante were going to drive out and see what was going on. The second message I got is the one you're really not going to like. It was from Roxanne."

"Tell me Roxanne went with Dante and Mom," Pierce said through gritted teeth.

Tuck's mouth formed a thin line as he shook his head. "Wish I could, but she didn't."

Pierce's stomach plummeted. "Where is she?"

"She called to say that two of her men showed up claiming Sweet Jessie was down and needed immediate attention. She called to let us know that she'd be leaving with them."

Pierce drew in a shaky breath. "Did she say which two of Roxanne's men?"

"Toby and Ethan."

Could it get worse? Pierce forced himself to think. "Call the sheriff's dispatcher and see what they know of Maddox's accident."

Already dialing, Tuck held the phone to his ear and waited, then asked the dispatcher what was going on. A moment later his face looked even more grim. "They never called Mom."

"See if you can get Maddox on the phone."

"You know cell phones have little to no reception out that far."

"Try."

Tuck hit speed dial for Maddox's cell phone with no luck, then Dante's.

"We have to get there faster than driving." Pierce jerked the steering wheel to the right, sending them south.

Tuck held on to the armrest. "Where are you going?"

"The airport."

"We won't get a plane out that fast."

"We're not going by plane, if we can help it.

Dial your friend Rick Knoell, tell him it's an FBI emergency."

"We don't have clearance from our supervisor," Tuck said even as he glanced down at his phone.

"If it was Julia, would you question it?"

Tuck searched his contacts list and selected one, holding the phone to his ear. "Rick, I need another favor. I know, we've been making it a habit. This is important. We need to get out near Medora ASAP."

Pierce listened to the one-sided conversation, holding his breath.

"Can you be ready in ten minutes? Thanks." Tuck shook his head and hit a number on his speed dial, glancing across at Pierce. "I should make you place this one."

"Who are you calling now?"

Tuck sighed. "Our boss. He's not going to be happy."

"Give it to me." Pierce took the phone from Tuck as their supervisor answered.

"Radcliff speaking."

"Pierce Thunder Horse, sir. We've made a command decision to appropriate the use of a helicopter to get us to the badlands in a hurry."

"Better have a damn good reason," Radcliff barked.

"Sir, I believe we may have narrowed down the NorDak Militia weapons stash we lost track of on the raid two months ago. We might need backup should things go south."

"Then you should wait until I can call in the ATF."

"Sir, no sir. There's a possible hostage situation that won't wait. I believe we can get in and lock down the location before the militia catches wind that we're coming." He paused. "With your permission, sir."

A long pause ensued as Pierce pulled off the highway at the airport exit and sped toward Rick Knoell's hangar. If he had to, he'd pay Rick out of his pocket for the use of the helicopter.

But if his gut had this right, this was a bigger can of worms than even he had originally anticipated.

"If you're wrong…" Radcliff started.

"I know, it'll come out of my pocket." Pierce maneuvered the truck into a parking space and shifted to Park.

"That's not all that you'll lose."

"I'll risk it, sir. I have a gut feeling." Pierce shifted the phone to his other ear and switched off the truck.

"We need more than a gut feeling."

"Sir, given the last operation, I think we have a better chance of rounding up the weapons without fanfare and joint ops." Pierce held his breath. He'd go without permission, but having it would help.

"If I didn't trust you, I'd say you're risking a helluva lot." Radcliff snorted. "Hell, I trust you and I *still* think you're risking a lot."

Pierce opened his door and climbed out, still holding the phone.

"Do it," Radcliff commanded. "Keep me informed."

"Yes, sir." Pierce hit the off button before Radcliff could change his mind, and he tossed the phone to Tuck.

Tuck shook his head. "Why did you just tell the boss you'd found the weapons?"

"Because I think we have." Pierce jogged toward the hangar, Tuck keeping pace. "Think about it. Someone shot at Roxanne when she got near to the canyon. When she tried to go down into the canyon with Jim, they were stopped with a landslide."

"What about when you two were in the canyon that night it rained?"

"Maybe there were too many people around to get away with anything at the time. We had cover as we descended to the canyon floor. The rain kept us from exploring too far."

"What about the fire in the barn?"

"I'm not sure, but I have a hunch." Before he could elaborate, they were pulling out their FBI credentials and showing it to the lady at the desk of the helicopter courier service run by pilot Rick

Knoell. Rick was out on the tarmac finishing up his preflight check.

"Ready?" he asked, sliding into the pilot's seat.

"Let's go." Pierce climbed into the front seat and settled the headset over his ears.

"Where exactly are we going?" he asked.

"The badlands north of Medora." Pierce closed his door and settled back. "Can you hurry? It could mean the difference between life and death."

ETHAN JERKED THE RIFLE to the left. "Get in the cave."

"Why?" Roxanne stalled.

"Just do it." The young man's lip lifted in a sneer. "Just because you own a ranch doesn't make you better than anyone."

"I didn't say it did."

"People like you lord it over regular folk, making our lives miserable enough until we want to do something about it."

"When did I make your life miserable?" Roxanne walked slowly up the incline to the cave's entrance. Oddly enough, now that she was faced with the man who might have been responsible for the attacks against her, she felt calmer than she had the entire week. Maybe it had to do with finally having someone in front of her that she could deal with directly, not having to wait and worry about when danger would strike. Maybe it was just that Ethan was someone she knew— someone she might be able to talk down from whatever crazy plan he'd formed.

"I hired you to do work on a ranch. You said you'd done ranch work before. Did I ask you to do anything I wouldn't have done?"

"You're like the rest of them," Ethan muttered, his eyes wide, his hands shaking.

Roxanne stopped in front of him, wondering how she'd get through to him when he looked so unstable. "Who is 'them'?"

"Shut up!" He poked her in the belly with the end of the rifle. "Just get inside."

"I'd like to know what I've done that warrants being yelled at and prodded with a rifle."

"You poked around where you shouldn't have."

"And where was that?"

"Here in the canyon, damn it!" He grabbed her arm and jerked her into the cave.

Roxanne stumbled and righted herself. "It's part of my ranch—why wouldn't I go into the canyon?"

"Because that's where we keep this…" He waved his free hand at the stacks of boxes lining the cave walls. On top of and beside the boxes were military rifles, grenade launchers and machine guns, all shiny and new.

Roxanne's stomach flipped over as she stared

around the interior of the cave, lit by a single gas lantern. "Good Lord, how'd you get all this in here?"

Ethan smiled. "The badlands can hide a lot, if you know where to go."

She shook her head, stunned by the amount of equipment. "I don't get it. I live on this land, and I don't remember seeing anyone coming in and out of the canyon."

"Because we didn't want you to. We moved it at night."

"But why do you need it? What's the purpose?" Her gaze landed on a long fat tube that looked like a World War II bazooka. She wasn't sure exactly what it was, but knew it could probably inflict a lot of damage. "You could supply an army with this much stuff."

"Exactly. It's the beginning of the end of a government that is no longer run by the upper-class minority."

"What are you talking about?" She faced Ethan, trying to make sense of what she saw and what he was saying.

"The silent majority, the working-class people are taking back our government from people like you who think you own everything."

Roxanne laughed, in spite of the tension of the situation. "I don't own everything, I'm struggling to make payments on what I have. What does this have to do with you holding a gun on me?"

"My job was to keep anyone from discovering the cache." He shook his head. "But you just couldn't stay away from the canyon."

She tore her gaze from the stockpile. "You were the one that shot at me. I should have known. You disappeared often enough, when you should have been working." She nodded at a dirt bike leaning against the wall in the corner. "You're pretty good on a dirt bike, but thankfully a lousy shot. So why bring me here if you didn't want me to find this cache?"

"To kill you." Ethan's words rang out against the cool stone walls, his eyes a colder gray, the gun leveled on her.

Now she was starting to get scared. The air left Roxanne's lungs and she struggled to keep it together in the face of imminent danger. "Kill me? Why? What have I done to you?"

"Other than poking around in the canyon, not anything worth dying for."

"Then why me? Why now?"

"It's not so much what *you've* done, it's what your *boyfriend* did." His voice dropped low, echoing in a low hum off the cave walls. "And I didn't know who your boyfriend was until yesterday."

"What are you talking about? I don't have a boyfriend."

Ethan waved the rifle wildly. "Bull! I saw you two practically crawling into each other's skins."

Roxanne stood with her hands planted on her hips, facing Ethan, refusing to show her fear in the face of his threat. If he was going to shoot her, he'd have to shoot her face-to-face. "That doesn't mean we're together. We split up two months ago, after my brother died."

"Yeah, after he killed my girlfriend."

"What?"

"You heard me. Your boyfriend was responsible for killing my Leah."

"How?"

"His raid on that warehouse set off the explosion. He got there too early. Leah was inside. She shouldn't have been in there when it went off. The feds were supposed to come later, after our people got out. But no, your boyfriend ordered them in earlier. It's his fault. Pierce Thunder Horse killed Leah just as if he'd stuck a gun to her head and pulled the trigger." His body shook, his voice cracking as tears filled his eyes.

"Oh, Ethan. I lost someone I loved in that raid, too." Roxanne stepped toward him.

"Stay back."

"Listen. You don't have to do this." Roxanne reached out. "Please, Ethan, let me have that gun before it goes off."

"That's the idea." He shoved the gun at her

hard, the barrel hitting her in the rib, making a snapping sound.

Pain lanced through her where metal smacked against bone. Roxanne doubled over, clutching her rib cage. "Ethan, hurting me won't bring Leah back." She pushed her words through gritted teeth, fighting to hide the pain.

"I know that." He swiped his empty hand across his face, brushing aside his tears. "What do you think I am, stupid?"

"No, I don't. I think you're grieving and lashing out at anyone you can, because you're still hurting." Like she had.

"Shut up." Ethan fired off a round.

The bullet missed Roxanne, tearing into a wooden crate.

"Ethan, you're not a killer." Roxanne struggled to keep the fear out of her tone, to be firm yet gentle. "Put the weapon down and let me help you."

"No. It's over. I'm tired of hiding, tired of guarding this stuff, tired of being told what to do. I just want Leah back."

"Ethan, she's not coming back." Roxanne shook her head, turning sideways to provide the narrowest target she could if he decided to shoot again.

"It hurts. Missing Leah hurts so bad." His tears spilled over and ran down his cheeks, the rifle shaking in his hands. "Your boyfriend needs to know what it feels like to lose the woman he loves."

"You'd hurt me to punish Pierce?" She straightened, though it hurt to. "Pierce didn't send Leah into that building. She went in there on her own."

"They weren't supposed to move on the building until Leah got out, but they did, because of Pierce."

"What happened is done, Ethan." Roxanne inched toward the man as his tears continued. If she could get close enough, she might be able to grab for the gun. "Don't make it worse."

"It wasn't supposed to happen that way. Leah wasn't supposed to be there, or stay that long. She was supposed to get out before…"

"Before the explosives went off?" Roxanne whispered, recalling her own anguish over losing her brother, Mason.

"Yes!" Ethan jerked the gun. "They weren't supposed to get there that soon. Not until she got out. Not until it was time."

"What time was that?"

"The specific time I tipped them off with, damn it! The ATF and FBI agents were getting close to the truth. I wanted them to raid the empty warehouse, to set off the rigged explosives and get rid of them. It wasn't supposed to happen like it did. Leah wasn't supposed to die, and because she did, you will, too."

"Ethan—" Roxanne started.

"Shut up and turn around." Ethan demanded, jabbing her again with the barrel of the rifle. "I'm going to kill you and when Pierce comes to find you, I'll kill him, too."

No. Roxanne couldn't let that happen. No matter what happened to her, Ethan couldn't go after Pierce. And, she realized, she couldn't die without letting Pierce know how much she still cared for him. She had to tell him that she didn't blame him anymore, and that he shouldn't blame himself. No matter what had happened during that raid at the warehouse, Pierce hadn't been responsible for Mason's death. She'd known that all along, even though she'd refused to admit it, wanting to have someone to blame.

But what had happened over the past couple days had made her realize life was short. She could die in a car wreck or be thrown by a horse. When your number was up, it was up, no matter how you went out. The most you could hope for was to love someone with all your heart for as long as you could and be thankful you had that time together.

She refused to believe her time with Pierce had come to an end.

A surge of adrenaline and determination shot

through Roxanne and she made a grab for Ethan's rifle, knocking the barrel to the side.

The gun went off, the bullet pinging against the wall of the cave, ricocheting back at them.

Roxanne dropped to the dirt.

The bullet hit Ethan in the shoulder, knocking him backward so hard that he hit the cave wall and crumpled to the ground, the rifle falling to the ground in front of him.

Tears welled in Roxanne's eyes as she staggered to her hands and knees and scrambled across the floor, reaching for the rifle.

As her hand closed over the stock a black boot landed in the middle of her hand, pinning it.

"Leave it," a heavy voice said.

Roxanne shrieked and jerked her hand free, sitting down hard on the cave floor as she turned to stare up into the barrel of a semiautomatic pistol.

Chapter Fifteen

"Can this thing go any faster?" Pierce leaned forward as they skimmed across the plains heading west.

"I'm giving it everything I can," Rick's voice crackled over the headset into Pierce's ears. "Look down. That should be the Thunder Horse Ranch we're passing over now. Where to from here?"

"Head for the canyon." Pierce pointed toward the wide, scarred swath of broken earth.

As they neared the edge of the canyon, Pierce leaned over, peering down at the land below. "See that pond?"

"At one o'clock?" Rick nodded. "Yup."

Disappointment washed over him as he stared at the deserted ground around the pond. No sign of Roxanne, Ethan or Toby anywhere to be seen. That didn't deter him. Pierce would use the tracking skills his father had taught him to find them. "Put us down close to the canyon rim."

As the chopper lowered over the land, Pierce could see a cloud of dust rising from the east and another in the west. Riders, heading their way. If they'd gotten his messages then it was probably his brothers from the east and Roxanne's men from the west. They wouldn't get there for several more minutes. Minutes he couldn't waste waiting for backup. He had Tuck. His brother was a trained agent and they both carried their guns. It would have to be enough to start with.

He prayed to *Wakan Tanka* that they didn't run into the entire militia in their efforts to bring Roxanne home alive.

As the helicopter skids brushed the ground, Pierce threw open the door, jumped out and ran toward the watering hole, Tuck racing to catch up.

Fresh tracks led away from the pond toward the edge of the canyon, veering to the north, instead of descending at the old trail.

Tuck caught up with Pierce. "Only two horses. Julia said Roxanne left with Toby and Ethan."

His chest tightened. "We have to assume she's with Ethan, and that he's dangerous."

Pierce followed the tracks to an outcropping of rocks and boulders where they vanished. The ground was rough, made of plate rock swept clean of dust and dirt. Horses wouldn't make tracks on solid rock. He'd lost the trail.

ROXANNE HELD UP A HAND as if that would stop a bullet from killing her. As her focus shifted from the gun's barrel to the man holding it, she gasped. "Deputy Duncan? Oh, thank God you're here. Ethan tried to kill me."

The deputy didn't reposition the weapon. "He'd have saved me the effort."

"What?" Roxanne had trouble wrapping her mind around the deputy's words. "What do you mean?"

"If Ethan had done his job right in the first place, no one would have found this cave."

"I don't understand. You're an officer of the law."

"Yeah, and I'm tired of crap for pay and the government taking a huge chunk of what little I make in taxes. Taxes that go to building bridges to nowhere and investing in companies that take jobs out of the United States. We plan on retaking our country."

"By force?"

"It's the only way."

"And you're going to use this stuff to do it?" Roxanne waved her hand around the cavern. "I assume you're part of the militia Ethan was talking about."

"Damn right I am." Shorty glanced around at the stacks of weapons. "Ethan really screwed up. He should never have shot at you in the first place. It only brought more attention to this canyon. Now we can't get the weapons out without drawing even more scrutiny from the Thunder Horses. The FBI will get involved and, if they put the pieces together, the ATF will be back in the mix. It'll be a damned warehouse fiasco all over again. Had I known Ethan was responsible for tipping off the FBI about the warehouse, I'd have killed him sooner."

Roxanne shook her head. She'd heard the warehouse raid hadn't netted the number of weapons anticipated. "Were these the weapons moved before the warehouse raid in Bismarck?"

"Yeah, and now, because of you and Ethan, we're back to square one. I'll have to bury the weapons to keep the feds from finding them and discovering my part in it."

Roxanne knew that his plan to keep his link to the militia a secret meant he'd have to get rid of her. She scooted backward, trying to get as far away from his gun as possible.

"Yeah." Shorty's eyes narrowed. "You and the idiot will be buried with the weapons." He raised his arm, pointing the gun at Roxanne's face.

She grabbed the only thing she could find in reach, a loose stone, and flung it at Shorty's hand. It missed, glancing off his cheekbone, but it was enough to distract him from shooting as a trickle of blood ran down his neck.

"Damn you!" Clutching a hand to the wound, his lip curled into a snarl and he aimed at her again.

Roxanne's life passed before her eyes as she waited for the bullet. The one thought that stood out above all others was an image of Pierce on horseback, his cowboy hat shading his eyes, a smile across his face as he rode toward her. Back when they couldn't be apart for long, when their love had been untainted, fresh and new.

She wanted it back. Wanted Pierce's love. Wanted to tell him that she loved him and had never really stopped loving him, even when she'd called off their wedding.

Now she sat on the floor of a cave, staring death in the face, wishing she had one more chance to tell Pierce how she really felt.

A loud click echoed against the cave's walls, but the bullet didn't come.

Roxanne scooted back farther, bunching her knees beneath her.

"You're not getting away from me." Shorty pulled the trigger again. Click.

Roxanne jumped to her feet and flew at Shorty, hoping to startle him into dropping the weapon altogether, giving her time to escape.

Just before Roxanne collided with Shorty, he raised his pistol and slammed it down on her head.

Pain bolted through her skull, clouding her

vision as her body crashed into Shorty's chest, knocking them both to the ground.

Roxanne rolled to the side and tried to rise, but blood ran into her eyes, blinding her.

Another blow to the side of her head and she was done, collapsing face-first into the dirt, swallowed by the black void of unconsciousness.

"THEY CAN'T HAVE DISAPPEARED." Pierce dropped to his haunches and scanned the ground, hoping to find a horsehair, droppings...something... anything that would lead him to Roxanne. "Their trail is somewhere close by. It has to be." He rose and rounded the outcropping of boulders protruding up and spilling over the edge of a rocky cliff. The boulders formed a maze of giant obstacles, with gaps around and between. Desperate for some sign, some indication as to where the horses had gone, Pierce entered the maze and wound his way through a corridor wide enough for a horse or an ATV.

As he emerged on the other side, he discovered a trail leading down into a part of the canyon he had never explored. As he descended a few feet down the stony path, the ground grew more dusty and he could make out tracks of horse hooves... and a dirt bike. "Tuck, down here!"

"Down where? Where are you?" His brother's

voice sounded muted and distant, the boulders muffling his words.

Pierce hurried back through the maze to where Tuck stood. "Come on. There's a trail wide enough for horses. And I found the tracks of a dirt bike."

"What about the others on their way? How will they find us in this?"

Pierce yanked his shirt over his head and draped it on the boulder most visible from the pond, in case the others looked that way. Rick Knoell had seen the direction they'd headed, so he'd point the others in the right direction. Once they reached the boulders, they'd find the trail he'd leave on the stones. Pierce dug in his pocket for change. As he led the way through the maze, he dropped quarters, dimes and nickels to indicate the correct path.

As they emerged on the crooked trail leading down into the canyon, Pierce drew his gun, holding it at the ready.

The trail wound up and over ridges, in and out of boulders that had fallen halfway down the sides of the cliffs, leading them deeper into nature-carved valleys, ravines and crevices.

When they emerged on the canyon floor, Pierce hugged the walls, weaving in and out of giant boulders that had once been a part of the cliffs above. Pierce could understand why they hadn't discovered this area before. The horses and cattle would find little or no food in the rocky ravines. But someone wanting to hide would find plenty of places in the caves dotting the cliffs, especially the ones closest to the ground.

He stopped beside a giant stone the size of a house and looked up at the dark holes in the cliff walls, some high up, others near the canyon floor.

Tuck moved abreast of Pierce, who was peering over his shoulder. "Which one do you think they're in?"

Pierce scanned the darkened entrances. "I don't know, but they have to be inside one of them." He nodded to the other end of the deep crevasse. "They wouldn't have ridden out that way. Too steep."

Again the ground turned stony and tracks were hard to follow. Once he left the shelter of the boulder, he would be exposed to anyone holding a gun. "Stay here and cover me," he said to Tuck, and took off running toward the cave with the largest entrance of those on his left.

No shots rang out as he climbed up the slope toward the gaping maw.

The first cave proved to be no more than an overhang, barely large enough to hide a man and a horse, much less two horses. As he slipped down the slope and moved on to the next cave, he heard a voice. He inched toward the entrance.

The voice continued muttering and the scuffling of shoes across loose gravel carried to Pierce.

Someone was inside.

Adrenaline kicked in, sending him up the slope faster. As he neared the entrance, he scooted to the side, plastering himself to the wall, scanning the ridges and cliffs around him, searching for sharpshooters or sentries to warn those inside of intruders.

Nothing moved, no sun glinting off metal or field glasses. Pierce waved for Tuck to join him. Backup would be important if he hoped to get to Roxanne, especially going into a dark cave after being in the bright sunlight. He closed one eye, preparing for his move into the darkness. He prayed he wouldn't be too late.

He gave Tuck a thumbs up and covered for his brother as he headed his way.

PAIN RICOCHETED OFF THE inside of Roxanne's head, forcing her back to the world of the living. She blinked once, then twice, willing her eyelids to remain open.

The darkness that greeted her made her think she was still asleep. As her vision came into focus she realized she was lying on her side next to a wooden crate. She wasn't in her nice soft bed, but on the cool stone floor of a cave.

The events that led her there rushed in on her

and she tried to sit up. She couldn't move. Her hands and feet were duct-taped together in front of her. Another piece kept her lips from moving. Near the mouth of the cave, Shorty Duncan, the deputy with a dark secret, reached as high as he could, pushing claylike lumps against the rocks.

It had to be some kind of plastic explosive material.

Roxanne didn't have much time. If she wanted to get out of the cave alive, she couldn't lie there all trussed up.

She wiggled her way to the corner of one of the crates and rubbed the tape binding her wrists against the coarse wood. A strand at a time, the tape broke free. She kept an eye on Shorty during the process.

When he glanced her way, Roxanne played dead, her body going limp, her efforts ceasing until Shorty went back to his work preparing to bury her alive. He pressed wires and something metal into the malleable substance, stringing them together.

When Roxanne had her hands free, she hurried to pull the tape free from her ankles and mouth, timing her movements with Shorty's to mask the sound.

A groan rose from nearby where Ethan lay against the wall. His hand moved to the wound on his shoulder and he groaned again.

Roxanne held her breath, hoping Shorty wouldn't hear him and come to investigate. At least until she could climb to her feet and run.

Ethan beat her to it. He lurched to a standing position. "What are you doing?"

Shorty turned to face Ethan. "I'm burying the cache, thanks to your stupidity."

Ethan staggered forward a step. "And you were planning to bury me with it?"

His lip curling into a snarl, Shorty glared at Ethan. "I wouldn't have to sacrifice our hard work if it hadn't been for you going on some revenge kick."

"I loved Leah. Those Thunder Horse brothers killed her."

"No, you did that yourself, by tipping them off."

Ethan opened his mouth.

Shorty jabbed a finger at him. "And don't try to deny it. You were the one who told the FBI where to find us and got our people inside the warehouse killed. If you want to blame anyone, blame yourself for Leah's death."

Ethan's face darkened, his breathing growing more erratic. He threw back his head and roared, charging at Shorty like a drunken bull.

Shorty braced himself, but it wasn't enough.

When Ethan hit him, he slammed against the wall of the cave, his head hitting hard.

The two men fell to the ground.

With Shorty and Ethan occupied, Roxanne pushed to her feet and scrambled for freedom. As she neared the entrance, she could see the sunshine and practically feel it on her skin.

A hand snaked out and locked on to her ankle.

She tipped forward, her momentum slamming her into the cave floor. Her vision blurred, a gray haze closing in around her. Roxanne refused to give in, refused to pass out and die in the cave. She pushed against the floor, rolling over as Ethan flung himself at her.

Barely avoiding him, she rolled out of reach and shoved to her feet, only a few steps away from escape.

Ethan leaped up, grabbed her hair and jerked her to a stop, his arm clamping around her neck.

Roxanne kicked and struggled, but Ethan's hold remained firm, cutting off her air.

"I want Pierce to know how it feels to lose the one he loves," Ethan said.

With the little air she could squeeze past his hold, she said, "Pierce doesn't love me." Her heart broke at her own words.

"Yes, I do, Roxanne." A silhouette filled the cave entrance. "Ethan Mitchell, let go of her, or I swear on the Great Spirit, I'll rip you apart."

"Pierce?" Roxanne cried out, the sound cut off

as the arm around her neck tightened, lifting her until her feet no longer touched the ground.

She dug her fingers into the arm, scratching and clawing for oxygen to refill her starving lungs. Her chest hurt, her vision started to blur as her arms weakened. It was over—she didn't have the strength to fight anymore. But Pierce had said he loved her. Pierce Thunder Horse had said he loved her. She had everything to live for. Dying was not an option.

A surge of hope filled her body and sent a flash of adrenaline through her system. She let herself go limp, playing dead, letting the full weight of her body land on Ethan's arm—the arm still injured from the shot he'd taken to the shoulder.

Ethan staggered back, his grip loosening.

Roxanne jabbed her elbow into his gut as hard as she could.

He released his hold and Roxanne dropped to the ground.

Pierce charged across the floor in a linebacker stance, plowed into Ethan, and sent him flying into the stack of wooden crates.

The impact knocked the wind out of the injured man and he crumpled to the floor, his hands clutched around his ribs. "Damn you, Thunder Horse. Damn you to hell." He rolled to his side, reaching for his rifle.

Pierce kicked it away from his hands. "Enough.

You've caused enough problems. Give it up." He jerked Ethan to his feet and twisted his arm up behind him. Leaning close to the other man's ear, Pierce spoke in a clear, intense tone. "I'd have killed you for what you did to Roxanne, but that would have made me no better than you."

"You killed Leah," Ethan cried.

"No." Roxanne pushed to her feet. "*You* did by leaking the information to the FBI. You knew the warehouse was wired to blow. It was your call that killed Leah and my brother, Mason."

Pierce shoved Ethan forward. "I'm sure there's a prison cell with your name on it."

"Don't be so sure he'll make it that far."

Roxanne spun to face Shorty Duncan.

The man held a metal box in his hand. He blinked the blood out of his eyes and staggered backward toward the entrance, his hand reaching for a toggle jutting out of the top of the box.

"He's got the detonator!" Roxanne yelled, diving for the man, knowing she'd never reach him in time.

Another form appeared behind Duncan, yanking the box from his grip before the deputy could flip the switch.

Shorty rounded on the man behind him, reaching for the detonator. "Give me that."

Tuck Thunder Horse pistol-whipped Shorty against the side of his head, sending the deputy flying backward. The older man tripped over a boulder and landed flat on his back. When he tried to get to his feet, Tuck pointed his gun at the man. "Stay where you are. I've lost all patience for the local law enforcement, so don't try me."

Roxanne found the duct tape and bound Ethan's wrists behind his back while Pierce held him steady. Then, with a great sense of justice, she bound the deputy's wrists behind his back, as well. She wanted to slap a piece across his mouth, but resisted the payback urge and tossed the roll to the ground.

She led the way out of the cave, letting the sunlight warm her face and her insides. So much had happened, everything spun inside her head.

Maddox and Dante had just crested the ridge overlooking the crevasse where the caves were hidden. As they dropped down to the canyon floor smiles spread across their faces.

Mattox chuckled. "I see you didn't need our assistance after all."

Tuck emerged from the cave dragging Shorty Duncan behind him.

Dante's eyes rounded. "Well, well. What have you got there?"

"One of the leaders of the NorDak Militia and an entire cave full of weaponry." Tuck tossed the detonator to Dante.

Roxanne ducked, her body tensing, anticipating the explosion.

Tuck chuckled. "Don't worry, Roxanne. I pulled the wires loose from the explosives.

Roxanne let go of the breath caught in her throat and laughed shakily. "Don't scare me like that."

Maddox dropped down out of his saddle. "Need a hand there, brother?"

Pierce pushed Ethan Mitchell into Maddox's grip. "Take him, will you? I need to get Roxanne home. She's been through a lot."

"Take my horse. I'll catch a ride in the helicopter."

Roxanne's heart skipped a couple beats as Pierce hooked her arm. Suddenly shy, she pulled back, avoiding the showdown with Pierce Thunder Horse, afraid it would be their last. More afraid that what he'd said wasn't true. He really didn't love her.

Tears welled in her eyes, her head pounded where the deputy had hit her and she didn't have the strength left to keep from telling this man just how much she loved him. "Leave me alone, Pierce," she said, then turned to walk away.

"Damn you, woman." Pierce caught up with her and scooped her legs out from under her, crushing her to his chest. "You will stop running from me and listen to what I have to say. After that, if you still want to leave, I'll let you go."

Tears slipped from the corners of her eyes. "I don't want to hear it."

"You damn well better." Pierce shook his head, his own eyes glazing. "Why are you crying? You know I can't stand it when you cry."

"Because…because…oh, hell, because I love you and I was stupid and…well…now you know. And you're not in any way obligated to love me back. Even though you said you did in the cave when you thought I was going to die. I love you, Pierce Thunder Horse, and I'd just as soon die if you don't love me back—"

Pierce's lips closed over hers, stemming the gush of words spewing from her mouth.

Chapter Sixteen

A round of applause erupted behind Pierce as his tongue slid past Roxanne's lips, between her teeth to connect with her tongue.

Her arms circled his neck, drawing him closer.

Wakan Tanka had to be smiling down on him. Roxanne was alive and in his arms. He'd found all the happiness he needed in this kiss. If he could freeze a moment in time, it would be this one.

As his head lifted, reason returned with the air filling his lungs.

"Why did you kiss me?" she asked, her tears glistening on her cheeks.

"To shut you up." Tuck chuckled as he led Shorty Duncan past the pair. "Never heard a woman say so little with so many words."

Roxanne swung a hand at Tuck. "I can still whip your butt, Tuck Thunder Horse."

"You'll have to get in line behind Julia. She has full rights as my fiancée."

Pierce glared at Tuck.

"What?" Tuck looked all innocent.

"Stop flirting. You're practically a married man."

"Then do something about her." Tuck pointed at Roxanne. "She's trouble."

Pierce's gaze captured Roxanne's. "I know. More than you can imagine."

Roxanne looked down first. "You can put me down, you know."

"What if I don't want to?" He held her tighter.

She inhaled and let the air out in a short burst. "Why, Pierce? Why won't you let me go?"

"Because I almost lost you. I'm afraid if I put you down, I might lose you all over again."

Roxanne waved at the men climbing up over the ridge, leaving them alone in the canyon. "No one's shooting at us. You and Tuck took care of the bad guys."

"They aren't the ones I'm afraid of." Pierce let her feet fall to the ground.

Roxanne didn't move out of his arms. She stood close, her hands resting against his chest. "You're afraid? Of what?"

He gripped her arms, staring down at her, his body tense, his heart pounding. "That I should let go of you...but that I won't be able to."

Her hand cupped his cheek and she shook her head. "You don't make sense."

Pierce let go of one of her arms and captured her fingers with his. "I'm not the right man for you, Roxanne."

Her lush, full lips thinned into a straight line. "Then who is? And don't give me that crap about someone who will be around for me. I can take care of myself."

He started to shake his head, but she jumped in before he could say anything.

"Okay, so I needed a little help when I had someone gunning for me. But that's not something that happens every day. I've been running the Carmichael Ranch for four years, and up to this point, I've had no problems. I can do it again."

"But—"

"But what? You don't trust me since I was the one who called off the wedding?"

"No, I understand why you did that. Believe me, I blame myself for Mason's death as much as you do."

"Stop." Roxanne held up a hand. "You said it yourself—the one to blame for the explosion is Ethan. He's the one who set the explosives and sent your team in. You need to stop blaming yourself."

"I got the tip. I should have seen it as a setup."

"None of the agents did—why should you? I don't blame you for Mason's death."

Pierce smoothed a strand of hair out of her face. "Mason asked me to protect you. How can I do that when I know that an FBI agent's wife is never safe from waiting and worrying if her husband is going to come home?"

Roxanne frowned at him. "Is it that you've had time to think about us and realized you couldn't live with a sometimes long-distance relationship?" She pulled out of his arms. "I can understand and accept that." She turned and started to walk away. "Don't worry about hurting my feelings—I'm a tough girl. Besides, I have to get back to work. I have a ranch to save from the bank."

"Roxanne Carmichael, sometimes you talk too much." Pierce caught her before she got two steps and spun her to face him. "My problem is that I love you *too* much."

"You sure have a way of showing a girl." She reached up to wipe the tears from her face.

He captured her hand before she could brush away a single tear and thumbed the moisture from her cheek. "It's not fair to ask you to wait for me, to be alone so often. Like you said...you have a ranch to run. I go where and when the bureau sends me. We'll always be going in different directions."

"So, you're letting me go. Fine. Let go." She glanced pointedly at his hands.

Pierce shook his head. "I can't." He pulled her into his arms and rested his cheek on her head. "You're so much a part of me, I can't function without you. I'll give up the FBI, if that's what it takes to be with you."

She pushed against his chest. "You'd give up the FBI for me?" Her lip trembled and she sucked it between her teeth. "No way."

"Yeah, I would. I'll turn in my resignation as soon as I get back to the office."

She shook her head. "You can't."

"Why?"

"Because I love you." Roxanne stood on her toes and pressed a kiss to his lips.

Pierce held her at arm's length. "Now you're not making sense."

"I couldn't live with myself knowing you gave up a job you love for me." She smiled up at him. "I'll sell the ranch. I could follow you wherever the FBI sends you, or be waiting when you get back." Her brows furrowed. "If you want me to."

Pierce hugged her to him, his heart full of his love for this woman. "We'll figure it out, sweetheart. Somehow, we will."

"Does that mean we'll be together at least some of the time?" she said into his chest, her fingers curling into his shirt. "Please say it does," she whispered.

"It does." His arms tightened around her.

Roxanne's hands circled the back of his neck and she tipped her head up to stare into his eyes. "Will you marry me, Pierce Thunder Horse, even though I canceled on you before? I promise I won't this time."

A chuckle rose up his throat. "Yes, I'll marry you. But shouldn't I be the one asking?"

"Does it matter?" She leaned into him, pressing her lips to his.

No, Pierce thought. It didn't matter as long as they were together.

"HERE LET ME HELP YOU with that." Mrs. T. took the veil from Roxanne's hands and slipped it over her head, anchoring the comb in her hair. "There."

Roxanne stared at herself in the mirror, amazed at her own transformation. She smiled, her eyes filling with tears. "My mother would have loved being here. She always wanted to see me in a dress."

"What?" Julia slid up beside her and stared into the mirror, patting her own veil. "Didn't think you had it in yourself to get all dolled up in a wedding dress?"

Her cheeks burned. That's exactly what she'd been thinking. "I'm just surprised I can still fit into it."

"Like you were going to gain any weight rounding up a couple hundred head of cattle and loading them onto trucks. That's about as likely as you finding time to eat while dealing with the bank, making a couple trips back and forth to Bismarck and giving statements to the FBI and ATF, and—in your spare time—planning a wedding over just a couple of days." Julia dragged in a deep breath. "Whew! I'm tired just listing it."

Roxanne laughed. "You make it sound... chaotic?"

"It was." Julia hugged her, grinning.

"I'm just glad the bank decided to renew my mortgage. When I get the check from the cattle sale, I'll be okay."

"What a relief after all you've gone through." Julia hugged her again. "I'm so glad you agreed on this double wedding."

"Me, too." Roxanne liked Tuck's fiancée and was glad she'd be around at family gatherings.

"And to think I didn't want to marry Tuck because he was an FBI agent." Julia shook her head. "And here I am, about to do just that."

Roxanne tucked a strand of her red hair into the bunch of curls secured to the top of her head. "What changed your mind?"

Julia smiled. "I thought I couldn't live with him, knowing he could die at any minute. But I realized I couldn't live without him, and would rather have as much time with him as I could get. And Lily deserves to know what a wonderful father she has." Julia stared across at Roxanne. "What changed your mind?"

"Pretty much the same reasons." Roxanne chuckled. "Even when I was being pigheaded, I never stopped loving the man."

Amelia laughed. "My boys can be pretty pigheaded, too."

Katya entered the room, a smile lighting her eyes. "You two look so lovely." She pressed her hands together. "I cannot wait for my own wedding to Maddox."

"It's too bad you couldn't join us." Julia crossed the room to hug Katya.

Roxanne smiled. "Julia, you're going to run out of hugs at this rate."

She laughed. "I'm delighted to be a part of such a big family. If not for Tuck and the Thunder Horse clan, it would be just me and Lily." Her smile faded. "I miss my sister so much."

Roxanne fought the ready tears that had been bubbling to the surface since she'd woken up that morning. "I miss my brother, too."

Katya sighed. "I would have loved a simple wedding, here on the Thunder Horse Ranch. But that is not to be. My brother insists we marry in my country."

Roxanne grimaced, imagining the crowds and required decorum. "Sounds like a lot of pomp and circumstance."

"Of which you will all partake." Katya stood tall and commanding in a way only royalty can pull off without looking arrogant. "I insist that the entire family come to Trejikistan for the wedding."

Roxanne hugged Katya. "I'd love to. I'll have to clear it with my husband, though." She grinned, almost pinching herself over the use of the word *husband*.

"I'm sure he'll agree." Amelia and Julia took turns hugging Katya.

"Hmm, someone's missing." Roxanne glanced around the room. "If all the women are in here, who has Lily?"

Julia's lips turned up on the corners. "Tuck volunteered to take over diaper duty while we got ready. I wonder how he's holding up?"

"I CAN'T GET THIS BOW tie to look right." Tuck yanked it loose yet again.

"What's wrong, brother, getting cold feet?" Dante lounged in a chair across the room.

"Shut up, Dante. You'll be next at the altar, after Maddox." Pierce held Lily carefully so that she didn't spit up on his tuxedo.

Dante shook his head. "Not if I can help it. I like being a bachelor. Kinda like the last man standing. Footloose and fancy free."

"You just haven't met the right woman," Tuck said. "I give up." His hands dropped to his sides.

"Here, let me." Maddox took over, and in a few quick movements had Tuck's tie perfect.

"How is it that the cowboy knows how to tie a bow tie and the fed doesn't?" Dante teased. "You'd think with the undercover activities you guys participate in, it would be a requirement to know how to tie a bow tie."

"Guess I missed that training session at Quantico." Tuck smiled. "Thanks, Maddox. You doing okay over there with the little one, Pierce?"

Pierce nodded. "She's an angel." He liked the way Lily snuggled against him and how warm and soft she was. His heart squeezed in his chest as he wondered what his and Roxanne's babies would look like. Would they have red hair like Roxanne or the dark straight hair of their Lakota ancestors?

"It's about time. You two ready?" Maddox crossed to the door and held it open.

"You bet." Pierce's pulse quickened. He handed Lily over to Tuck. "I believe this sweetheart belongs to you."

"Hey, Lily. Let's say you and me go to a wedding." Tuck straightened his little girl's pretty white dress, dropped a kiss on her cheek and stepped through the door. No hesitation.

Maddox clapped a hand onto Pierce's back. "Any second thoughts, little brother?"

Pierce shook his head. "Not one." He'd loved Roxanne for so long, marrying her would only make his world complete. Still, he couldn't believe it was actually going to happen.

Maddox's brows dipped. "You look a little nervous."

Pierce's lips twisted. "Until I get a ring on her finger, I won't believe she's really going to marry me."

"Kinda the way I feel about Katya." Maddox sighed.

"And you have to go all the way to Trejikistan to tie the knot." Pierce clapped a hand on his brother's back. "I'm glad the ladies decided on home for this shindig."

"Shall we?" Maddox held the door.

"I'm ready." Pierce led the way, emerging into the great room of the Thunder Horse Ranch house. The space had been transformed into a garden with flowers and greenery strategically draped over the mantel, wooden beams and walls. The huge leather couch had been moved to one of the bedrooms, replaced by a couple rows of white wooden chairs, decorated with cheerful white daisies, ribbons and yellow roses.

All of Roxanne's ranch hands were present, except Ethan, who had spent the past couple days in jail in Bismarck with Shorty Duncan. A contrite Toby stood with his cowboy hat in his hand, still mentally kicking himself for being played the fool by Ethan.

Pierce chuckled at how uncomfortable the cowboys looked all duded up in freshly pressed jeans, crisp white shirts and neckties. Every one of them tugged at the constriction, probably counting the minutes until the ceremony was over and they could lose the ties while digging into the catered barbecue brisket and cases of beer.

Pierce's stomach rumbled as the rich aroma of smoked brisket and roasted corn drifted to him from the kitchen, reminding him that he hadn't eaten breakfast.

He took his place beside Tuck and Lily in front of the fireplace, tugging his jacket and checking the placement of the single white rose on his lapel. At least he had on his black cowboy boots, instead of the patent leather dress shoes the tuxedo shop had tried to rent to him. Thank goodness Tuck had been in agreement with him and chosen to wear the same.

Music filled the room from the piano their

mother had tried unsuccessfully to get all the boys to play at one time or other. She'd arranged for one of the young men from the Medora Musical to play for the ceremony.

As the music swelled then faded, Pierce shifted beside Tuck, starting to worry that Roxanne would get cold feet and regret her decision.

Then the wedding march filled the air and Julia emerged from the hallway and floated toward them, smiling.

Tuck adjusted Lily in his arms and stepped forward to take Julia's hand. "You're so beautiful," he whispered as he turned toward Hal Jorgensen, the local justice of the peace, who'd come out to perform the ceremony.

Pierce held his breath, his gaze riveted to the hallway, his hands clenched at his side.

Then she stepped from the shadows, her deep red curls piled high on her head, her long, slim neck bare all the way down to the dip of her cleavage into the strapless wedding gown that hugged her figure like a glove.

Pierce froze, his heart stopping as her gaze met his. He'd never seen a more beautiful woman, and she was about to become his wife.

As she moved toward him, his chest tightened and his heart kicked in, shooting adrenaline throughout his body. He let go of the breath he'd been holding and hurried forward to take her hands in his. *"Cante waste nape ciyuzapo."* He pressed one hand to his chest. "I greet you with my heart."

Roxanne's smile lit the entire room. "Did you think I wasn't coming?" She took his elbow and squeezed. "Didn't you know?" She stared into his eyes and took a deep breath. "I'm going to mess this up, but here goes… *Mitawa cante itawa niye.*" She looked up, hopefully. "Did I get that right?"

Pierce grinned, his chest swelling so full he thought it might explode. "Yes, if you were trying to say, 'You got intoxicated on the way to the market.'"

Roxanne's eyes widened and she pressed a hand to her mouth. "Is that what I said?" She laughed. "I was trying to say my heart belongs to you."

"Pierce." His mother's voice reminded him he was standing in a room full of people, waiting for the wedding to begin.

"You said it right, and…" he brought Roxanne's hand to his chest "…*mitawa cante itawa niye.* Forever."

She blinked back tears.

Pierce inhaled and let out a steadying breath. *"Wakan Tanka yuha yuwakape miye."* His hand slipped around Roxanne's waist and he pulled her to him as they stepped toward their destiny. "The Great Spirit has blessed me."

* * * * *

LARGER-PRINT BOOKS!
GET 2 FREE LARGER-PRINT NOVELS PLUS
2 FREE GIFTS!

Harlequin®

INTRIGUE®

BREATHTAKING ROMANTIC SUSPENSE

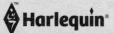

FAMOUS FAMILIES

YES! Please send me the *Famous Families* collection featuring the Fortunes, the Bravos, the McCabes and the Cavanaughs. This collection will begin with 3 FREE BOOKS and 2 FREE GIFTS in my very first shipment— and more valuable free gifts will follow! My books will arrive in 8 monthly shipments until I have the entire 51-book *Famous Families* collection. I will receive 2-3 free books in each shipment and I will pay just $4.49 U.S./$5.39 CDN for each of the other 4 books in each shipment, plus $2.99 for shipping and handling.* If I decide to keep the entire collection, I'll only have paid for 32 books because 19 books are free. I understand that accepting the 3 free books and gifts places me under no obligation to buy anything. I can always return a shipment and cancel at any time. My free books and gifts are mine to keep no matter what I decide.

268 HCN 0387   468 HCN 0387

Name _____ (PLEASE PRINT) _____

Address _____ Apt. # ____

City _____ State/Prov. _____ Zip/Postal Code ____

Signature (if under 18, a parent or guardian must sign)

Mail to the **Reader Service:**
IN U.S.A.: P.O. Box 1867, Buffalo, NY 14240-1867
IN CANADA: P.O. Box 609, Fort Erie, Ontario L2A 5X3

FFBPA12